JUDITH BLEVINS & CARROLL MULTZ

EYEWITNESS

A NOVEL

OPEN WINDOW

Livonia, Michigan

Published by BHC Press
under the Open Window imprint

Library of Congress Control Number: 2018946735

ISBN: 978-1-947727-71-7

Visit the publisher at:
www.bhcpress.com

Also available in ebook

CONTENTS

A NOTE FROM THE AUTHORS

It has been said that the criminal justice system is less than perfect. Although it is the prosecutors' duty to seek justice, not necessarily convictions, the prosecutors are oftentimes placed squarely in the middle in exercising their prosecutorial discretion. Sometimes they resort to grand juries to make charging decisions and other times leave it up to their own best judgment and hope a trial jury will validate their decision to prosecute.

If a prosecutor is in office very long he or she will have alienated a majority of the electorate and if he or she is wise will think twice about running for office at the next election cycle. It is easy to understand the rationale behind this statement. If the prosecutor fails to obtain a conviction, the victim and the victim's friends and family will be outraged. If the prosecutor obtains a conviction, the defendant and the defendant's friends and family will be outraged. Ultimately, everyone will be outraged.

At one time, eyewitness or direct evidence was thought to be superior to circumstantial or indirect evidence. All of this changed with the development of DNA analysis and the release from prison of those who scientifically couldn't have committed the crime for which they had been convicted. Unfortunately, scientific evidence is not always available in every case.

It's a fact that law enforcement focuses on building a case against those they are convinced committed a crime. This is usually done on the perceived strength of the case and the likelihood that their target is the perpetrator. Although criminal trials are designed to convict the guilty and acquit those unjustly accused, it doesn't always work out that way. And on the basis of the reputation of the victim and his or her status in the community versus that of the accused, the former's credibility will trump the credibility of the latter almost every time.

As the saying goes, "It is better that ten guilty men go free than one innocent man be wrongfully convicted." We both aspire to that adage. But it still begs the issue as to who is telling the truth—the accuser or the accused. Credibility is usually a jury question and it is a known fact that the jury is not always correct in its assessment.

The authors leave it up to the reader to determine whether eyewitness testimony is the most reliable and what verdict the reader would have rendered had they been on the jury that made the decision in the case featured in this novel.

Our thanks to our publisher, BHC Press and to Margie Vollmer Rabdau whose contributions made this novel what it is.

This novel is dedicated to those wrongfully accused and those who rally in their behalf.

Justice delayed is justice denied.
~ William E. Gladstone ~

PROLOGUE

I look up as Deputy Warden Henderson approaches my cell. He's carrying a large manila envelope. I'm surprised when I see him because the normal procedure for receiving mail is that a correctional officer distributes the incoming mail to the inmates in the dayroom in the early evening. At mail call, if your name is called, you receive your mail by showing your ID. It's very unusual to have personal delivery.

I walk over to the bars that separate my cell from the corridor. "Evening, Deputy."

"Hey, Monty," he says, and slides the envelope through the bars, "Warden said this looked too official to wait for mail call. He wanted me to get it to you as soon as possible."

I accept the envelope and examine the return address. It's from the State Medical Board of Ohio. I instinctively know what's inside. "Thank the Warden for me, Deputy," I say without looking up.

"Sure thing, Monty. Hope it isn't bad news…"

I don't hear the rest of what Henderson is saying. I slowly turn toward my bunk. My knees are weak, my heart is thumping and I suddenly find it hard to breathe. I sit down, and with shaking hands, I carefully lift the flap on the envelope and extract the contents.

State Medical Board of Ohio
30 East Broad Street, 3rd Floor
Columbus, OH 43215
March 30, 2018

Montel Rudland
c/o Ohio State Penitentiary
878 Coitsville Hubbard Rd.
Youngstown, Ohio 44505

Re: Revocation of license to practice medicine in the
State of Ohio

Dear Dr. Rudland:

The State Medical Board of Ohio, at its monthly meeting, reviewed your case. Attached is a copy of the minutes pertaining to your plea…

I hurry through the ten pages of minutes and pull the last page from the stack. It reads:

A vote was taken on Dr. Rudland's motion requesting the board delay its decision to revoke his license to practice medicine in the State of Ohio until such time as all of the appeals pertaining to his criminal case have been exhausted.

ROLL CALL:
Dr. Ritchie - abstain
Dr. Sudermann - abstain
Dr. Otway - nay
Dr. Pierston - nay
Mr. Pindar - nay
Dr. Manzoni – nay
Mr. Leland - aye
Dr. Faraday - nay

Dr. Conrad - nay

Dr. Castlewood – nay

The motion to delay suspension of Dr. Montel Rudland's license to practice medicine in the State of Ohio is denied.

It is recommended his license be revoked immediately.

I read the letter again. Since the beginning of the ordeal, my life has been moving so fast that I'm unable to comprehend all that is happening. *How the hell did I come to this time and place?*

PART ONE

THE JOURNEY BEGINS

CHAPTER 1
ROYAL FLUSH RANCH

Hawarden, Iowa, a small town located approximately fifty miles from Sioux City, has a population of around twenty-five hundred. The Rudland homestead was acquired by my Great-Great-Grandfather, Edger, somewhere around the turn of the century. It is said that he won a six hundred and forty acre prime section of land in a poker game, and eventually increased it to two thousand five hundred and sixty acres, or four sections.

The story handed down from generation to generation is that the beautiful preacher's daughter, Claire Lancaster, was sought after by all the eligible men in and around Hawarden. The two top contenders were my Great-Great-Grandfather Edger Rudland and Billy Atkinson, the son of a wealthy property owner, Wilson Atkinson. The Atkinsons had a mansion in the middle of their ranch, and they were revered and envied by other ranchers in the vicinity.

Wilson, determined to teach his four sons the value of hard work and the dollar, divided his two thousand five-hundred and sixty acre ranch into four sections, deeding a six hundred and forty acre section to each of his four sons. Not unlike the landowner's stewards that are depicted in the book of Matthew, the sons were held accountable and obligated to increase their wealth annually. Vying for their father's favor, the brothers became fierce competitors.

As was the custom in those days among the settlers in that part of Iowa, Sunday was strictly reserved for church and family and the Atkinsons abided by the custom. The other six days of the week the Atkinson boys worked like the devil fattening their herds and growing feed for the winter reserve. However, Saturday night was their night to howl. They would ride their horses into Hawarden and congregate in the local salon. They were not the least bit shy about flaunting their wealth, but were also generous, often buying drinks for the house. They were very popular and well respected by the town's folk.

THE OLD TIMERS TELL the story of Great-Great-Grandpa Edgar and Billy Atkinson's feud as follows: One Saturday morning Wilson summoned Billy into his office knowing how his son liked hobnobbing around Hawarden.

"Son, we need some supplies from town. Your mother is running low on flour and other staples. She asked me to send you to town to get them."

"Yes, sir!"

"Thought you'd say that." Wilson handed Billy a list scribbled on the back of a tobacco ad, saying, "Here's the list. You should be able to find everything at Berman's Mercantile. Have Mr. Berman charge it to our account."

"Yes, sir!" Billy exclaimed.

Wilson rose to walk Billy out, but before he could get to the door, Billy, in his exuberance, was astride his horse and headed for town. Wilson shouted after him, "Be careful!"

The warm sunny day bolstered Billy's good mood. His spirits were high as he jostled along the dirt road leading into Hawarden. When Billy approached the outskirts of town, he noticed several people gathered in the graveyard adjacent the church. Out of respect for the dead, he dismounted, removed his hat and walked his horse past the mourners as was the custom. He kept his head lowered as he passed the cemetery, but would occasionally glance in their direction.

Although Claire played for church services, Billy hadn't paid much attention to her as she was usually hidden behind the high organ. That day, when he saw her at the gravesite, something in him stirred. She was the picture of femininity in her pink and white gingham dress. The wide-brimmed straw hat that framed her angelic face was tied in a pink bow under her chin. Long blond curls poked out from beneath the hat and bounced about when she moved and her blue eyes sparkled in the morning sun. At that moment, Billy's world was forever changed. *That's the girl I'm gonna marry.*

It is said that Great-Great-Grandpa Edger was of the same mind. He was acquainted with Claire through attending church services. Although no pistols were involved, the duel between Billy and Edgar for Claire's affection was on. Those in the know told of how Claire was undecided which beau to choose. Although Edgar was just starting out, he was confident and determined to buy some land and make his spread the best in the Midwest. He was far better looking than Billy, however Billy brought wealth and security to the table. The boys doted on Claire and showered her with trinkets. She was smitten with both beaus and refused to commit to either one. The two pursuers eventually became frustrated in their quest to claim Claire's hand in marriage.

One Saturday night, so the story goes, Billy had had too much to drink. Hopeful to eliminate the competition for Claire's hand, he challenged Edgar to a one-hand winner take all poker game. The stakes were high; Billy put up his section of the land his father had given him in return for Edgar's promise to back off in his pursuit of Claire. Billy's brothers tried to reason with him but Billy was stubborn. Having boisterously made the bet, his honor prevented him from backing down.

Folklore has it that when the cards were revealed at the end of the hand, Edgar held a royal flush to Billy's three aces/ two kings full house. It is told a stunned Billy buried his head in his hands and wept. He was too ashamed to have to admit to his father how foolish he had been, so instead of going home, he rode off into the night and was never seen or heard from again. There was some speculation that he went to Kansas City, but that rumor was never confirmed.

The next day when Edgar called upon Claire to ask her to marry him, it is told, she was as mad as a wet hen. She was overheard shouting at him, "I'm humiliated, embarrassed and insulted that you agreed to use me as a stake in a poker game. Furthermore, I wouldn't marry either one of you if you were the last two men on earth!" She then slammed the door in his face so violently that some of her mother's dishes fell from the open shelves in the cupboard.

THESE EVENTS TOOK PLACE in 1917, just as America was entering World War I. When our country entered the war, twenty-four million men born between 1873 and 1900 registered for the draft. My family is, and always has been, among the original Bible thumping, flag waving, red-blooded Americans who fought and died for our right to do so. Rudland history is recorded between the pages of the wars that ensued between 1914 and 1945.

The story goes that Edgar, not having any family to speak of and being unable to cope with being turned down by Claire, enlisted in the Army. He is said to have proclaimed, "My country's been good to me and I owe it to future generations to see that our way of life is preserved."

Edgar spent most of his tour fighting on the battlefields in France, and upon showing extreme heroism, was promoted to sergeant. He led his unit with valor and distinction. He was even reckless with his own life, plowing headlong into situations no normal human would even consider. He fought as though he had nothing to live for and seemed to want to accomplish all he could for his country before he died. Upon suffering a grave injury on the battlefield, he was transported to one of the Army field hospitals. It is said that he was in and out of a coma for several days.

When he finally opened his eyes, a nurse by the name of Viviana Prescott, who was later celebrated as a hero herself for her unselfish sacrifice to care for the wounded on the battlefield, was there beside him. She was so angelic, his first thought was that he had died and gone to heaven. The story goes that his vision of her changed when she began to change his bandages and he writhed in pain. It is said she stayed at his bedside day and night.

They fell in love and by the time Edgar left the hospital, they were married. Edgar returned to America a war hero with his lovely Viviana at his side. He was given a hero's welcome at the Hawarden train station.

Sadly enough, it is told, Wilson Atkinson lost his three sons at the Battle of the Somme on the Western Front. To this day it's unknown what became of Billy, he never returned. Wilson, a lonely, brokenhearted old man, was among the throng that met Edgar and Viviana at the train station. He pushed through the crowd and pulled Edgar aside, requesting Edgar pay him a visit the next day.

When Edgar and Viviana approached the Atkinson spread, they noticed how poorly it had been maintained. Edgar was surprised as the Atkinsons were the pride of Hawarden before the war. Wilson met them at the door and ushered them into the dusty parlor. He was an honest man, and advised Edgar that he wanted to pay Billy's debt. When he handed Edgar the deed to Billy's portion of the ranch, Edgar, just as honorable, refused to take it. It is said Edgar insisted he pay for it. Over the years, Edgar had saved over five hundred dollars and offered it to Wilson as payment for the section of land.

The storytellers say that Wilson was moved to tears. He was in poor health, and having lost his wife a few years before, asked Edgar and Viviana to stay and oversee the spread. Since they had no other place to live, they agreed to the arrangement. Viviana took over the running of the house and nursed Wilson back to health. Edgar turned the spread into the biggest and best in the county. At the end of his life, Wilson deeded the entire ranch over to Edgar. And that's the story of how the Rudlands acquired the two thousand five-hundred and sixty acre *Royal Flush Ranch.*

CHAPTER 2
THE LOVE OF MY LIFE

Our family has maintained the *Royal Flush Ranch - Double Circle R* for over a hundred years. In fact, we've been here so long, the locals just refer to it as *The Old Rudland Place*.

Great-Grandpa Lawrence, one of Edgar and Viviana's six children, took over the operation of the *Royal Flush* when Great-Great-Grandpa Edgar succumbed during the flu epidemic in 1943. Edgar was only forty-nine years old when he died. Viviana's pioneer spirit enabled her to take the reins and keep the ranch afloat during the ensuing war years. A lot of food items were rationed and beef was in such great demand that it was even black marketed. The price of beef skyrocketed thus allowing Viviana enough income to support the children and measurably increase the cattle herd.

Lawrence married his high school sweetheart, Emma Wettington, and soon there were three more Rudlands running around the ranch. My Dad's father, Grandpa Andrew, was the only one of Lawrence and Emma's three children who elected to stay on the ranch. He was the son Lawrence called wild and woolly. Andrew never met a horse he couldn't break and his roping skills were unrivaled. It was rumored Andrew was good enough to be a rodeo star. However, Andrew chose to follow in the footsteps of his ancestors and stay on the *Royal Flush*. His marriage to Margaret O'Keith produced six sons, one of whom was my father.

Dad's five brothers couldn't shake the dust off their feet fast enough. As soon as they were old enough to strike out on their own, they gravitated to the larger cities and a more engaging life style. Dad loved ranching and chose to stay. My Grandpa Andrew is in his 80s and basically retired. However, he runs things from his recliner—or at least Dad lets him think he does. My parents, Maxwell (Max) and Willa, oversee the day-to-day operations of the spread, and Dad employs a crew to help herd the two hundred and ten head of cattle he runs year round. I loved growing up in the wide open spaces and I'm thankful Dad made the choice he did.

MY NAME IS MONTEL Rudland, but everyone calls me Monty. I was born in 1974 and was joined two years later by my sister, Sandy. Our brother, Danny, came along five years after Sandy. During those formative years, Sandy and I considered Danny a pain in the rear. Living on a ranch far from our nearest neighbor, Danny had no other children to play with and was constantly bugging us to entertain him.

Sandy and I finally agreed to a minimum of two hours a day between us. Sandy would play learning games with him and I would play basketball or football. Dad and I rigged up a child-size basketball hoop in the driveway and Danny seemed to relish the time we spent together. I was on the Kennedy High basketball team in Hawarden and taught Danny some of the Bengals' basketball maneuvers. I, of course, let Danny win every game. I watched him develop a healthy confidence and love for the sport. The same was true of football when he got older.

ALTHOUGH I LOVED BASKETBALL, football was my passion. I played first string all four high school years and my efforts were rewarded. I was awarded a football scholarship to the University of Iowa. That was the year the Hawkeyes won their division, and when I was a senior, I was featured on the cover of one of the 1996 editions of *Sports Illustrated*. Danny followed my lead, and after he graduated from high school, he went on to become a basketball star at the University of Iowa.

Sandy and I were close enough in age to be fierce competitors at the academic level. I have to admit she kept me on my toes. Even with my share of work on the ranch, football practice and Danny-time, I was determined that, even if it killed me, there was no way I was gonna let a girl, much less my sister, outshine me scholastically. Sandy also had her share of chores on the ranch plus cheerleading and track. Throughout our school years our grades were neck-and-neck, both maintaining a four point average. We unmercifully pushed each other to the limit of our abilities. If our parents suspected our intense competition, they never let that fact be known.

Years later, on her wedding day, as we danced to *Wind Beneath My Wings,* Sandy confided in me. Nodding toward the bandstand, she said, "I had them play this song especially for you. You were, and still are, the wind beneath my wings."

I was so surprised at her confession, I couldn't find words to reply, so I kept silent. She went on, "I hated you every day of my life." However, her words did not match her manner and I knew she was kidding. "Do you know why?"

"No why?"

"I never had a moment's peace following in your footsteps. With your exploits on the football field, I was determined not to let you get ahead of me academically. I felt I had to excel at something in order to be noticed. I was jealous of all the praise heaped on you by our parents and everyone else. I even killed myself participating in track and cheerleading hoping to rise up to your level. Even today everyone is still singing your praises."

My uproarious laughter caught the attention of other wedding guests and they stopped in their tracks and stared at us. We ignored them and hoped they would ignore us as well.

"You hated me? I despised you—for the same reason. You pushed me to the limits and beyond. I have you to thank for my football scholarship."

Not to be outdone, Sandy countered, "And I have you to thank for my being voted homecoming queen. But in my heart I knew it was because I was the sister of the football star."

Emotion welled up inside of me and I fought back the tears. "Sandy, I owe all that I am to you. You made me dig deep and find the strength and courage to do what, at the time, seemed impossible. It was *you* who put me on the cover of *Sports Illustrated*—"

I was surprised when Sandy suddenly pushed me away from her. "If you believe that, you're not the brother I struggled to emulate. You were my Superman, Batman, Spiderman and Terminator all rolled up into one. No superhero could live up to my image of you, you creep! Just accept the fact that you're truly special and the rock of this family."

Struggling to keep it light and not embarrass Sandy by blubbering on her wedding day, I said, "Well, there is that…"

I'll always remember that moment. Laughing and crying at the same time, Sandy and I clung to each other as we remembered the good times and the bad.

ALTHOUGH I LOVED RANCHING, I couldn't ignore the opportunity the football scholarship afforded me. Growing up, I assisted Dad as he administered to the sick and injured animals. I helped with the vaccinating, castrating and branding of our herd. I think, even as a lad, I had a desire to be a doctor. When that door was opened, it must have been fate that pushed me through.

I enrolled at the University of Iowa in 1992. Although the U of I was only three hundred and thirty miles from Hawarden, I'd never been away from home for any length of time and it felt strange being on my own for the first time. Iowa City, population seventy-four thousand, compared to Hawarden, population twenty-five hundred, was a whole new world. The enrollment at the U was ten times more than the entire population of Hawarden. I was the epitome of the country bumpkin for the first few months at the university. Eventually I dovetailed into the stream of things and didn't feel as though I stuck out like a sore thumb.

My football skills helped tremendously with the transition. Having wrestled steers all my life, I was one of the strongest players on the team and started as fullback. The coach soon realized my skills were being wasted and moved me into the quarterback position. That was where I wanted to be and that was where I excelled. Soon the Iowa City newspapers sports sections were carrying detailed stories of the Hawkeye's victories. Although I was in contention for the Heisman trophy, an injury prevented me from serious consideration.

Football came easy and I didn't have to kill myself at practice, and I devoted most of my energy to my academic studies. My burning desire to be a doctor spurred me on. In 1996, I graduated with a 4.0 grade average. My grades were so good, Dad, aware of my burning desire to be a doctor, at my graduation offered to pay my tuition in order for me to continue on to the University of Iowa School of Medicine.

"Dad! I don't know what to say."

"You needn't say anything, your actions speak louder than words." Dad punched me on the arm, "Besides, your mother and I need someone to take care of us in our old age."

I punched him back. "You may rack up the years but you'll never be old."

"Humph! Tell that to my aching hip."

We had a celebration feast at the Skyhigh in Iowa City. I had forgotten how much fun our holidays were when we were growing up. We laughed and cried and toasted each other late into the night. Even after giving birth to three children, Sandy was as beautiful as she was when she was cheerleading for Kennedy High School.

"Remember what a pain in the rear Danny used to be?" Sandy asked.

"Do I ever," I replied.

"Well, we just found out he's been accepted at Harvard. Little bro's going to be a lawyer."

"Get outta here!" I said.

"Yep," Dad chimes in. "We're gonna have a doctor and a lawyer in the family. Go figure. I just barely completed high school."

"Well, Maxwell," Mom says, "I've always known I passed the brain-genes onto the kids."

"No argument there," Dad mutters.

THE UNIVERSITY OF IOWA Carver College of Medicine is but three minutes from the main campus. I kept my apartment so when I returned to start the fall semester, I was established and ready to go. I can truthfully say that I loved every class and every minute of medical school. You'd think after four years of undergraduate school I'd be burned out, but not so. I relished my classes and looked forward to each day. Once again, I graduated with honors. The family decided to make celebrating at the Skyhigh a tradition and my celebration from medical school was even more of a bash—if that was possible.

HAVING LEAPED TWO HURDLES, I was ready for my internship. I applied to and was accepted by University Hospital in Iowa City. My first year was spent in General Practice and then I moved on to Family Practice Residency, a stage of graduate medical training where aspiring doctors practice medicine, usually in a hospital or clinic under the direct or indirect supervision of an attending physician. Although I was pushed to the breaking point during my three-year internship, I never looked back at my decision to become a doctor. Even enduring the grueling pace and sleepless nights, I loved every minute of it.

Midway into my residency, one of my fellow interns, Jesse Townsend, asked me to ride home with him. We were on the same shift and had the weekend off. Although Des Moines was less than a two hour drive, Jesse said he needed someone to help him with the driving.

"I don't trust myself to stay awake. I wouldn't even consider going except my parents are celebrating their thirtieth and it's a big deal to them. They'd be mighty disappointed if I didn't show."

"Sure, I'll go. In fact, getting out of Dodge for the weekend sounds like a pretty good idea."

I wasn't aware that Jesse's parents were filthy rich until we pulled into the driveway of a two story gray stone mansion located on Southern Hills Circle. The driveway seemed to go on forever winding through a perfectly manicured expanse of lawn.

A variety of trees, shrubs and flowers dotted the landscape and contributed to the fairytale-like setting.

Apparently noticing the expression on my face, Jesse said, "Dad did well during the real estate boom. Don't worry, they're still just downhome folks."

Once inside, and after all the greetings and introductions, I was given one of the six bedrooms and told to make myself comfortable. It was then that it occurred to me that I hadn't brought anything appropriate to wear to a fancy party. Although Jesse tried to accommodate me, his five foot ten, one hundred fifty pound wardrobe didn't cover much of my six foot three, one hundred eighty-five pound body.

"Hey, man. You're okay. Just relax, no one will notice."

Looking down at my worn jeans and U of I sweatshirt, I said, "Maybe I could just hang out in the kitchen…"

"Not on my watch. Stick close to me, I'll cover for you."

That's a weekend I'll never forget. Among the guests at the celebration were the Bundridges, owners of the local Mercedes-Benz dealership. Their daughter, Carissa, accompanied them. Jesse introduced us and when I took her hand in mine, I think I knew how Great-Great-Grandpa Edgar must have felt about Claire. I'd trade my horse and buggy for Carissa any day of the week.

"Happy to meet you." Then gesturing towards Jesse, she said, "Jesse and I have been classmates since the first grade."

"I, too, am happy to meet you," I managed, and couldn't help but look down at my attire.

Apparently noticing my discomfort, Carissa said, "Don't worry about sporting the U of I sweatshirt. There aren't too many Iowa State alumni here. And if you're attacked, I'll protect you."

That was when I knew she was the girl for me. She must have felt the same way about me, because when Jesse and I got back to Iowa City, I had a message from her.

"Call me!" And I did.

Our courtship was sporadic because of the hours I was required to work. However, we managed to spend a lot of time together and shared the traveling. I would go to Des Moines when I could, and when I couldn't, she would come to Iowa City. After I completed my residency, we were married.

The Bundridges must have spent enough on the lollapalooza to feed a third world country for a year. You'd think it was a royal wedding. After the ceremony, the toasting, the cutting of the cake and other traditional hoopla, we were finally alone.

I said, as I pulled her close to me, "Carissa, you look like an angel. You take my breath away."

"And you, Slugger," she whispered in my ear, "although you're quite handsome in that monkey suit, I think I prefer you in the U of I sweatshirt and worn jeans."

CHAPTER 3

THE MIGRATION

B ecause we were married as soon as I completed my residency at University Hospital, Carissa and I hadn't decided where we wanted to live. We considered somewhere in between Des Moines and Hawarden. However, in the midst of our decision-making process, I spotted an ad in the monthly Medical Journal. The Talman Medical Center in Cleveland was looking for a resident doctor.

I showed the ad to Carissa and raised my brows, "What do you think?"

"Perfect. I believe it's only ten hours from Des Moines and less than that from Hawarden. That's close enough for convenience but far enough away for privacy."

With Carissa at my side, I called for an interview. It was scheduled for the following Monday. We left Iowa City that weekend and drove to Cleveland to scope out potential houses, just in case. We were shown around the city by a real estate agent and when she took us to the Shaker Heights area and showed us a charming Antebellum mansion situated on two acres, both Carissa and I instantly made up our minds. That's where we wanted to live.

Dr. David Putnam, one of the founders of Talman Medical Center, interviewed me and hired me on the spot. With the help of our parents, Carissa and I were able to purchase the Antebellum in Shaker Heights.

We relocated to the Cleveland area, settled into our new home, and my career was taking off like a rocket. "Don't you think it's time we started a family," Carissa casually asked over breakfast one morning.

"Huh," I said and continued flipping through the morning paper.

"A family," she said. "You know kids…"

"Sure, whatever you want."

"You're not listening to me," she said. She then jerked the paper from my hands and slid one of those early pregnancy detection devices across the table. "Ready or not, here I come!" she said and pointed to the portion of the device that indicated positive for pregnancy.

It hit me like a bulldozer. "What…"

"I'll make it easy for you," she said, "you're going to be a daddy."

I remember jumping up and pulling her from her chair, twirling her around a few times.

"Easy, Slugger. Your son may be prone to motion sickness."

"Do you know if it's going to be a boy?"

"No, you're the doctor. However, I'll bet there's a fifty/fifty chance it will be."

"Don't care—I like girls, too."

Later that year, Jayden was born. Jennifer came along two years later and Paxton was a surprise, he was born five years after Jennifer.

PART TWO
THE ORDEAL

CHAPTER 4

THE ACCUSATION

It was approximately twenty miles from where I lived to where I worked. Living in an upscale neighborhood like Shaker Heights suited both Carissa and me and the school system in the Cleveland area was one we whole-heartedly endorsed. To have received a lucrative offer from a medical clinic of the caliber of Talman Medical Center fresh out of med school was a dream come true.

We never second-guessed our decision to leave Iowa—that is until our lives were turned upside down by a series of events I describe as the *ordeal*.

IT WAS A COOL balmy Saturday in October when Carissa came into the den and announced a detective with the Cleveland Police Department by the name of Summers was on the phone wanting to talk to me. Not knowing or even having an inclination as to what the call was about, I punched the mute button on the TV remote. *Nothing except a call from the CPD could interrupt a U of I football game—except maybe a call from a patient.*

"Hello!"

"Dr. Rudland?"

"Yes, speaking."

"Hate to bother you on the weekend, but the matter I'm about to discuss can't wait until Monday."

"Who is this?"

"Sorry. My name is Kevin Summers. I'm a detective with the Cleveland Police Department. You and I met during a Boy Scout Banquet a year or so ago. We received our Silver Beaver Awards together."

"Of course, our sons go to school together and received their Eagle Scout Awards about the same time. Is Marcus okay?"

"He's just fine, thank you. You, no doubt, have been reading about the series of break-ins in the Shaker Heights area."

"Yes. In fact I had a new security system installed just this past week. One of the nurses at the clinic had her home burglarized while she and her family were out of town not long ago and I was worried about all the break-ins. Is this what the call is all about?"

"I wish it was, Doctor. Unfortunately, that's not why I'm calling."

The hair on the back of my neck begins to rise. "Just call me Monty. I'll help anyway I can."

"I don't know if you remember a patient of yours by the name of Madeline Borchard. She's my sister."

I'm relieved thinking that's the purpose of the call. "Yes, of course. How's the fractured ankle holding up?"

"Couldn't be better. But that's not why I'm calling either."

"Sounds serious." *This cloak and dagger routine has me on edge.*
"It is."

Suddenly I'm anxious and blurt, "Not about my kids, I hope?"

"Absolutely not. It's about the break-ins. Is it possible Detective Reynolds and I could come by sometime today and speak with you at your home rather than disturb you at the clinic?"

"Yes, but I don't see how I can be of any help." *What the hell's going on?*

"It's not something we can discuss over the phone. Lloyd and I will be following up with a witness in your area at one and should be finished by two. Does two work for you?"

I glance at the TV, disappointed that I won't get to finish watching the game, as I say, "I'll make it work. You have my address?"

"Twenty-forty six Burnt Mill Road."

"Perfect. See you then." After I hang up, I stare at the phone for a few moments trying to figure out what role I could possibly have in this caper.

I LOOK UP AND notice Carissa standing in the doorway. "Wonder what that's all about?" I ask, as I tell her about the call.

"Doesn't sound as though it's about the Boy Scouts or the kids," she says. Anxiety tints her words.

At this point, the suspense is overwhelming and I press her for an answer. "Then what do you think it's about?"

"Beats me!" She snaps back and looks hurt. "I don't know any more than you. Maybe the break-in at the McKay residence. Stephanie may have used your name for some reason."

"Sorry, honey. I didn't mean to be so harsh" I say. "I thought of that, so I asked him about it. He said no."

Carissa sits down on the edge of my desk. "Maybe it's about our new security system."

"I also asked him about that and he said no."

Slowly spinning the letter opener in small circles on my desk, Carissa says, "Maybe they have a suspect who admitted to taking the items that are missing from our garage."

"All good guesses, but I reckon we'll find out soon enough."

WHEN THE DOORBELL RINGS, I meet Summers and Reynolds at the door. After Summers and I shake hands and exchange pleasantries, he introduces me to Reynolds. "This is Detective Reynolds," he says. Reynolds and I shake hands and I lead the two into the den, or what my friends and family call my man cave.

Looking around, Summers nods toward my display of awards. "Ever seen so many trophies and plaques?" he says to Reynolds.

"Only in a museum," Reynolds replies.

Reynolds studies the framed *Sports Illustrated* cover hanging on my wall. "I remember seeing that picture of you on the cover. Thought you were a shoo-in for the Heisman that year."

"That's kind of you to say," I glance across the room at the *SI* cover. "I knew that my chances were little to none when I broke my collarbone in the game against Iowa State."

"I remember that game," Reynolds says. "You were a marked man beginning with Iowa's first series of downs. That was pretty obvious with all the penalties against Iowa State for roughing the quarterback. Didn't think you'd survive even the first quarter."

"You and me, both! That was the defining moment. That's when I knew applying to medical school and not the NFL was a wise decision." I shift my weight and instinctively rub my left hip, saying, "The hip injury I received my freshman year still plagues me, not to mention the effects of some rather vicious tackles throughout the years."

"In light of all of your injuries, I'm surprised you're letting Jayden play high school football," Summers says, and moves further into the den.

"You can't keep them in a bubble," I say. "They'll grow to resent you. Speaking of which, you must be a little nervous about your own son. I hear Marcus needed some sutures after the last game."

"You hit the nail on the head. Like Jayden, you have to let them do their thing," Summers says.

I point to two stuffed leather chairs positioned next to my one-of-a-kind antlers coffee table. "Make yourselves comfortable." I take a seat on the matching sofa facing them. "Can I get you some coffee or a soft drink?"

"Coffee with cream and sugar," Summers says, placing a file and legal pad on the coffee table. "My caffeine level is getting low. How 'bout you?" he says and looks at Reynolds.

"Make that two!" Reynolds says, and puts an accordion file on the table next to Summers' file.

What the hell! All of these official looking files are making me nervous. When I go into the kitchen, Carissa already has a tray set up with three cups, sugar, cream and an assortment of pastries. She fills the cups with steamy coffee and whispers, "Hope it's just a social call."

"Can't tell," I whisper back. "But I'm feeling like a bug under a microscope."

When I enter, Summers and Reynolds reposition their files to accommodate the tray.

"Hey, man! That's first class service," Summers says, rubbing his palms together.

We each take a cup and select a pastry from the tray. Long minutes pass before anyone says anything, then Summers and Reynolds begin to speak at the same time. Reynolds points to Summers and says, "Why don't you go ahead?"

Summers nods, and taking a draw from his cup, swallows hard and says, "Where to begin." He opens a bulging file and pulls out the top sheet.

I still don't have a clue as to what this is all about. When Summers' demeanor changes, and he becomes all business, I become worried.

"I mentioned on the phone that there have been a number of break-ins in and around the Cleveland area. Without any real leads, we're checking every possibility." Summers scans the page he pulled from the file. "Recently, there was a break-in here in Shaker Heights. The break-in was on McCallum Boulevard only a few miles from where we're sitting."

I'm now on full alert, as his reference to the proximity bothers me. "Yes, I read about that."

"Then you know that the victim was a socialite by the name of Harriett Porter-Bingham. She was robbed at gunpoint when she startled the would-be burglar."

Maybe they're just wanting to know if I know the victim. "She's the heir of the mining mogul Morgan Porter," I say.

"And the widow of the late Percy Bingham whose grandfather founded the Bingham Department Store chain," Reynolds adds.

Summers is back on track, "Do you know her?"

"Only through reading the society section in the local newspaper." I wanted to add that we obviously run in different circles.

"Actually, she's the reason we're here." Summers raises his brows and peers at me.

That gesture is unsettling. "How so?" I ask, wondering how I fit into the equation.

"You see," Reynolds interjects, "Mrs. Bingham picked you out of a photographic lineup as the perpetrator."

I laugh, "Now I get it. This is a joke my colleagues have contrived to play on me."

"No joke," Reynolds snaps.

I'm stunned. "But I've never met Mrs. Bingham. How is it my photograph was in the lineup in the first place? I've never been in any kind of trouble."

Reynolds fields the question. "Mrs. Bingham described the perpetrator as a white male in his late thirties or early forties, at least six feet tall, weighing about one-eighty and clean shaven. We needed seven photos in addition to our number one suspect that fit the description. We had six of the seven photos and needed one more. Your photograph was taken out of your clinic's newspaper ad in last week's newspaper. When Mrs. Bingham viewed the eight photographs, she picked yours."

Still unsure this isn't a cruel joke, I flipping say, "Lucky me!"

Reynolds ignores my comment. "Summers said it was most unlikely that you were the perpetrator, and at his insistence, we withheld getting an arrest warrant."

I mouthed thank you to Summers. He nods and nervously shuffles the papers in front of him.

"So…where does that leave me?" I ask.

"Would you be willing to take a polygraph?" Reynolds asks and squints at me.

"You haven't asked if I did it," I say.

"According to Kevin, it's a case of mistaken identity."

"And to you?" I ask, as I fight to control my temper. I feel like a fool for treating this visit like a friendly encounter when, in fact, it's designed to pin me to the wall.

Reynolds fidgets. "With an apparent eyewitness, we can't just ignore the possibility. We're now forced to follow-up on the lead."

"Of course I didn't do it and yes I would be willing to take a polygraph."

Summers whispers something to Reynolds.

"Would you excuse us for a minute," Reynolds says. The two huddle in the hallway outside the den. After a few minutes, they return and Reynolds asks, "Would you be willing to participate in a live lineup?"

Without hesitation, I reply, "Absolutely. Why not? Your eyewitness is obviously visually impaired."

"We thought of that," Summers says. "That's why I suggested to Lloyd we interview you at your home and not drag you down to the police station and subject you to the prying eyes of the press and others."

Not to mention putting my medical practice in jeopardy. "I appreciate that," I say. "However, I'm disturbed by the fact that due to my name and photo recognition a person can just arbitrarily pick me out of a series of photographs and say I robbed her."

"That's why Kevin and I thought a live, or what we call the physical or police lineup, would be a more accurate method of identification since you were not a suspect until your photograph was the one Mrs. Bingham selected."

"It just makes sense that since she now has my face etched in her memory from the photo showing, it's inevitable she'll pick me in the physical lineup," I say.

"Not necessarily," Summers interjects. "That is always the fear. However, if the physical lineup is not unduly suggestive, it is the most accurate barometer of the two."

"Other than Mrs. Bingham's say so, was there other evidence, like fingerprints left at the scene, or maybe hair follicles or DNA?"

"Our lab is still analyzing evidence collected at the scene. It has only been a week since the break-in of Mrs. Bingham's residence," Reynolds says.

"And the perpetrator was wearing gloves and a baseball cap," Summers adds. Reynolds shoots Summers a disapproving glance.

"So much for fingerprints and hair follicles," I murmur. "It's beginning to sound like it's her word against mine."

"It would help if you had an alibi," Summers says. I feel like Summers believes my story and is trying to help. I'm not too sure about Reynolds.

"What was the date and time of the break-in at the Bingham's?" I ask.

"A week ago yesterday at some time around ten or ten-thirty p.m.," Reynolds responds.

"Well, I was at the clinic until sometime after six. Probably got home around seven or so. I—"

Reynolds stops me. "Maybe we should advise you of your rights in light of the ID and all." He looks at Summers. Summers shrugs.

Swell! After they extract all the information they can from me, it occurs to them to advise me of my rights.

Reynolds begins reading me my rights from a card he retrieves from his wallet. "You have a right to—"

I interrupt. "No need to read me my rights. I know what they are."

"Been watching the cop shows?" Summers asks, and smiles.

His smile does not reassure me. "And mystery novels—heavy with courtroom drama," I say.

"Need to read the *Miranda* warnings anyway," Reynolds says, "department policy." When he finishes, he asks, "Understand your rights?" Reynolds is now all business though not completely antagonistic.

"Yes," I respond.

Reynolds pulls a small recorder from his pocket and asks, "Mind if we record our conversation?"

"No," I reply. "I have nothing to hide." Besides, I figure I'm intellectually a few steps ahead of them and the more I cooperate the more likely they'll believe me.

"You started to say you arrived home at around seven on the night of the Bingham break-in." Reynolds takes the lead.

"Yes."

"What did you do then?"

I pause momentarily reconstructing the events of the previous Friday evening in my mind. "Well, I was pretty tired and hungry when I got home. I warmed up a dinner my wife left for me, and after I ate, I took a shower, then read for a while before falling asleep. I had a rough week at the clinic."

"Did you leave the house at any time during the evening or night?"

"No, I slept soundly until around six or six-thirty the following morning."

"Can your wife vouch for that?"

"Unfortunately, that was the weekend Carissa and the kids spent with Carissa's sister and her family in Akron. They left right after the kids got out of school sometime around three-thirty." *Dammit! This is probably the only time in my whole life I'd need an alibi.*

I watch Reynolds raise his brows and glance in Summers' direction. Summers just looks down and busies himself sifting through a sheaf of papers.

"Do you own any handguns?" Reynolds asks.

"Yes," I respond. "I have a Glock 17 that I've had a number of years that I keep in my desk drawer."

"Okay if we examine it?"

Don't know if it's the caliber of the questions or Reynolds' attitude, but I'm beginning to feel like I'm being railroaded. I stand and walk over to my desk which is located on the far side of the room. I'm surprised that neither one of the detectives follow me. Apparently, they're not too worried about their safety.

When I hand the gun to Reynolds, he examines it to make sure it's not loaded and hands it to Summers. "Here, photograph this." After it's photographed, Reynolds hands it back to me. "You can put this back in the drawer."

I replace the gun in the drawer and return to the coffee table. I deliberately remain standing, hoping the two will take the hint that they have worn out their welcome.

Without looking up, Reynolds says, "I just have one other matter to discuss. Do you have a coin collection?"

Along with everyone else who collected the state quarters. "Not much of a one," I respond. "Three sets of state quarters and some silver dollars is all."

Reynold's eyes light up. "Mind if we examine the silver dollars? According to Mrs. Bingham, the robber made off with some silver dollars that were minted in the 1890s. They apparently had some sentimental value."

As I again go to my desk, this time to retrieve a bag of coins, Reynolds adds,

"Her late husband apparently carried the coins in his pants pocket as had his father and grandfather before him. They were their good luck charms—at least according to Mrs. Bingham. Everything else of value was apparently kept in a safe deposit box. Except for a few hundred dollars in bills, little else was taken."

"Not a very lucrative night for the would-be burglar," I say as I hand Reynolds the bag of coins. He examines the coins and counts the silver dollars. "Twenty-three in all," he says as he hands them to Summers. "Photograph both front and back," he says. After the task is complete, he says to Summers, "Better photograph the bag as well."

"That's an old burlap flour sack that belonged to my grandmother. The bag with those old coins were given to me by my father. Notice none are worn as would be expected with the silver dollars taken in the Bingham robbery." There's no reaction by either Summers or Reynolds though I detect a slight smirk form on Summers' lips.

Reynolds and Summers gather their belongings and head for the door. On the way out, Reynolds turns and asks, "When would be a good time to have you participate in a lineup?"

"I usually take Wednesday afternoons off."

"We'll shoot for next Wednesday."

"Best you call me at home. Don't want to alarm my staff."

"I understand," Reynolds says. "We'll be as discrete as we can."

"Might want to talk to an attorney," Summers whispers in my ear as he follows Reynolds out the door. *Am I such a serious suspect that I need an attorney?*

As I watch them head for their car, I'm grateful they drove up in an unmarked police car and weren't in uniform. I have some very inquisitive neighbors.

I'd barely closed the door and started to walk down the hall towards the computer room where I knew I'd find Carissa when the doorbell rings. I open the door and find Reynolds standing there.

"Sorry to bother you again, but I neglected to ask whether you had a Cleveland Indians baseball cap."

Doesn't everyone this side of the Mississippi have one? "Yes, as a matter of fact, I do. Why do you ask?"

"The man who robbed Mrs. Bingham was wearing one."

"My two sons also wear one. Hopefully they're not suspects."

"A lot of us do," Reynolds says. "And from our standpoint no one is excluded as a suspect."

"Is there anything else you want to ask me?"

Reynolds shakes his head.

When I start to close the door, he blocks it.

"We'll probably have other questions later," he says as he keeps his hand on the door.

"If you think of more, just give me a call," I say. "I want to be as helpful as possible."

"We appreciate that," Reynolds says and smiles. "We're as anxious to prove Mrs. Bingham wrong as you are. Hopefully, we haven't disrupted your day too much." He turns and leaves.

Haven't disrupted my day--how about my life? If I weren't so worried, I'd laugh out loud at the absurdity of that last statement. When I close the door and turn around, Carissa is standing behind me. "What's with all the questioning?" she asks with a frown.

"Guess the police are just covering all the bases in trying to find a suspect in all the unsolved burglaries."

"Sounds more like they're trying to find a whipping boy, if you're asking me." Carissa places her arms around my waist. "Our three kids need a father and I need a husband. If you weren't around, no telling what would become of us—and your practice."

I had kept my composure pretty much up to that moment. I hadn't thought about what impact a mere accusation would have on my family, my clinic, my medical license, my reputation in the community, my parents reaction, my inability to provide for my family, my being convicted and going to prison, my position as president of the Ohio Medical Association, my standing with my church group, the Boy Scout Board and other organizations with which I'm affiliated, and I'd hate like hell to invade the college fund Carissa and I have set up for Jayden, Jennifer and Paxton to pay for an attorney to prove my innocence.

I let loose of Carissa and push her away. "You don't suppose..." I break down and cry.

CHAPTER 5

THE LINEUP

Our son Paxton comes in around five with his friend Logan in tow. I'm suddenly thankful our three children were otherwise occupied when the detectives were here this afternoon. Jennifer is spending the weekend with Amber Reed, her best friend and daughter of the deacon of our church. Jayden spent the afternoon working on a class project at school before going to his seven o'clock freshman basketball game.

"**WE NEED TO HURRY** if we're going to find a decent seat," Carissa coaxes.

"Do Logan and I have to go?" Paxton pouts. "Logan brought a new video game we want to try."

"Jayden would be disappointed if you weren't there, Pax," I say.

"Jennifer won't be there," Paxton persists, angling for an out.

"Amber's mother said she would be bringing Amber and your sister," I say. "Try again."

Paxton folds his arms defiantly, and slumping in his chair, whimpers, "Darn, I never get to do what I want."

I watch Carissa roll her eyes. "And with that attitude, you may even get to do less, young man. Now hurry it up!"

JAYDEN IS ALMOST A head taller than many of his team-mates and is a starter along with Summers' son, Marcus. The other team is no match for the Cubbies and by halftime there is no doubt as to the outcome. When I go to the concession stand, I run into Summers.

"The boys are looking good," Summers says, as he fumbles in his hip pocket for his wallet.

I order popcorn and soda for my group and hand the clerk a twenty. I'd offer to pay for Summers' order but I'd probably be accused of bribery. "The new coach and hard work are finally paying off," I reply.

When we turn and walk toward the stands, I notice Summers looking sheepish. "Sorry to cause you concern," he says. "Departmental policy, you know."

Sorry, my ass! I pull up short and Summers stops beside me. "Do you really think with the live lineup I have a ghost of a chance to avoid another misidentification—especially now that Mrs. Bingham has already made up her mind?"

"Guess we have to have faith in the system. Things have a way of working out."

"I hope you're right. The suspense is already taking its toll."

As Summers walks away with a tray of soft drinks and popcorn, he looks around and says in a soft voice, "Remember my advice about hiring an attorney?"

I nod and bite my lip. *Does he know something that I don't know?*

As I approach my seat, I'm spotted by another one of Jayden's teammate's father, Cameron Mackey. Cameron was a running back for Ohio State at the same time I played for Iowa.

"How the hell are you?" Cameron asks, patting me on the shoulder and spilling one of the drinks.

"Not so great!" I say, as I attempt to wipe the spill from my trouser legs.

Cameron offers to help, "Oops! Sorry about that." He looks up and examines my face more closely, "Looks like you haven't been sleeping. What's up, bro?"

I'm stunned that my appearance has deteriorated so much in just a few days. Following Summers' advice, I ask, "Your father still practicing law?"

Still studying my face, Cameron says, "He's of council now and has pretty much turned everything over to the young bucks."

"How can I reach him?"

"Just so happens…" Cameron pulls a card from his wallet and hands it to me. "Dad usually works only mornings. Give him a call Monday morning and he can point you in the right direction."

When I return to my seat and distribute what's left of the snacks, I'm somewhat relieved. Running into Cameron was a good omen and having Summers on my side, or so it appears, gives me a much needed edge. I slip the card Cameron gave me into my wallet. Before doing so, however I look at the name of the firm: *Mackey, Royle, Stone & Winthrop*.

On the way home, I ask Carissa if she's familiar with the name Winthrop.

"Why do you ask? Do you think you need a lawyer?"

"He's apparently a law partner in Cameron Mackey's father's firm. Somehow his name rings a bell, but I don't know how."

"His son, Leland Winthrop, is the one with all the high profile cases. He's the one who recently represented the senator charged with sexual assault. His wife, Bethany is in my Bible study class."

"Is he the same one who ran for prosecuting attorney some years ago?"

"That's the one. Bethany said if he hadn't been a Democrat he would have won."

"How old a man do you think he is?"

"Bethany is in her fifties so I would say he is about the same age, maybe a little older."

"And hopefully a little wiser. Hope he doesn't charge out the nose."

"You only get what you pay for," Carissa reminds me. "And hopefully this debacle isn't going to bankrupt us." Her statement is laced with sarcasm as well as concern.

FORTUNATELY MY MONDAY APPOINTMENTS are not stacked. At the first opportunity, I call the law office of *Mackey, Royle, Stone & Winthrop*. When I identify myself as a doctor, I'm immediately given a one o'clock appointment with Leland. I juggle my schedule and arrange to be at the law office at exactly one.

Upon arrival, I'm handed an intake form. I've just barely started to fill it out when the receptionist says, "Dr. Rudland, Mr. Winthrop will see you now."

"I haven't completed the—"

"That's okay. You can complete it later."

Guess having the title doctor has its perks. I remember even in med school we used the doctor designation to bypass not having reservations at some of the finer restaurants.

I'm led to Leland's office. He is on the phone when I enter. He motions for me to be seated in one of the leather chairs facing his desk. He is seated in a rather imposing high back chair. His physical appearance, clean shaven face, and well-groomed salt and pepper hair, remind me of what I envision a United States Supreme Court Justice would look like.

I look around the room while I wait. Lining one wall is a series of glass front bookcases with leather bound volumes that intrigue me. I cross the room and examine them. They are the early editions of the North Eastern Reporter containing cases from not only Ohio but the states of Illinois, Indiana, New York and Massachusetts. Leland places his hand over the mouthpiece and whispers, "Belonged to my grandfather."

I smile and nod. When I turn back to my seat, I notice the opposite wall is lined with framed certificates, plaques and photographs of Leland with various celebrities. His career is very impressive.

Leland, now off the phone, is standing. Gesturing, he says, "Those represent some of my most memorable defendants." When I shake his hand, I notice he is at least as tall as I am, maybe even taller and has a grip like a vise.

"Although our paths have never crossed," Leland begins, "I feel I know all about you."

"I take it you're a football fan."

"I am a fan. However, my source is my wife Bethany. She is always talking about a special friend who thinks her husband walks on water."

"That special friend wouldn't be a person by the name of Carissa and a member of your wife's Bible study group, would it?"

"Good guess. Did I give you too many clues?"

I never knew Carissa thought I 'walked on water.' I just can't let her and the kids down. I'm now even more devastated, but try to look relaxed. "Actually, it was Carissa who suggested I contact you."

"She has good taste—at least on three counts that I'm aware of. I'm curious why you scheduled an appointment with a criminal defense attorney and not an investment broker." He rounds his desk and we reposition the two chairs to face each other.

"The whole thing is embarrassing and absurd."

"Okay. Let me be the judge of that."

"Well, here goes," I say and take a deep breath. "Apparently, one of our clinic's ads in the newspaper was used in a police photographic lineup. My photograph along with seven others was shown to a victim of a break-in. Guess who was picked as the perpetrator?"

"That's an easy one. I can even tell you the name of the victim."

When I look at Leland with a quizzical expression, he says, "The only break-in that I'm aware of where the victim was home at the time of the attempted burglary is the mansion of the late Percy Bingham. Don't tell me you were fingered by Harriett Porter-Bingham?"

"You got it! Carissa said you were good. Maybe she's got her water-walkers mixed up."

"That's rich. I've been called many things in my day, but never a saint," Leland laughs.

"Apparently, my photograph was inserted as a filler and Harriett's identification was a complete surprise."

"The last time I saw her she was walking with a cane and accompanied by a nurse." Leland scratches his head. "She has to be in her mid to late 80s."

"The mansion is on McCallum Boulevard only a few miles from my home. My family and I have passed it many times on our bicycles. The mansion sits quite a ways back on the property and is surrounded by a twelve foot wrought iron fence. I'm sure it would have some kind of security system and not easy to breach."

"I'm familiar with it. Was there once at a fundraiser with my father when George Herbert Walker Bush ran the first time. It's quite a place. Maybe the fanciest home I've ever been in. A lot of silver and crystal."

Leland punches the intercom. "Brenda, see if you can find a copy of the newspaper article on the break-in at the Bingham Mansion. It would have been in either the morning issue of the Cleveland Bugle or the afternoon issue of the Gazette on Saturday, October fourteenth, the day following the break-in."

After he instructs Brenda to research the article, he says to me, "I remember reading the article in one of the rags. We usually keep the old editions a year or so in case we need to refer back."

"Good idea. Ours goes in the trash usually the same day unless there's an article we want to clip."

Leland leans back in his chair. "Monty, I take it you were contacted by the CPD."

"Yes. Eight days after the incident which was just this past Saturday." I try to look relaxed by mimicking Leland and leaning back, crossing my legs. "I was watching the IU game when Carissa came into the den and told me there was a Detective Summers on the phone wanting to talk to me. During our conversation, Summers informed me I had been picked out of a photographic lineup by Mrs. Bingham and identified as the person who robbed her at gunpoint on the night of October thirteenth."

"Friday the thirteenth," Leland says. "Not her lucky day and apparently not yours either. Hope you're not superstitious."

"Am now!" I say, and we both laugh.

"I assume two detectives showed up on your doorstep."

"Correct. Both Kevin Summers, who I knew, and a detective by the name of Lloyd Reynolds."

"I know Detective Reynolds. He's a fun one to cross-examine because he can never get his story straight."

When I raise my brows, Leland says, "For example, on one of my cases as he was identifying a series of items of clothing relating to a burglary, he repeatedly pointed to his initials that he had written on the items to establish they were one and the same as the ones he recovered. On cross, I had him point to the initials on a critical piece of evidence and show the jury. When he couldn't find the initials he had previously pointed to, his credibility went down the toilet."

"How about Kevin Summers?"

"Summers is a different breed. I've found him to always be truthful. How is it you know him?"

"Through the Boy Scout Advisory Board and our sons going to the same school and playing on the same basketball team. As they were leaving my home after the interview, out of the earshot of Reynolds, he suggested I talk to an attorney."

There's a knock at the door. "I have the newspaper with the article you requested," a stylish older lady with short-cropped gray hair and glasses says as she steps into the room.

"That was quick," Leland says as he stands and reaches for the newspaper.

"It was near the top of the stack," Brenda says with a smile and starts to leave.

"Meet Dr. Rudland," Leland says and gestures in my direction. "He was a star quarterback for the Iowa Hawkeyes." And to me, he says, "This is my secretary, Brenda Dickerson. She's the one who makes me look good."

I stand and shake hands with Brenda. "Pleased to see you again, Dr. Rudland," she says. "You don't remember me but I'm the patient with all the allergies."

"Of course," I say and give Brenda a big hug. "Didn't recognize you with the horn-rimmed glasses."

"Don't know what I'd do without Brenda," Leland says after she leaves the room. The newspaper had been folded to expose the article. He adjusts his glasses and reads out loud the contents starting with the headline.

WIDOW OF PROMINENT BUSINESS MAN ROBBED AT GUNPOINT

Harriett Porter-Bingham, heir to the Morgan-Porter mining fortune and widow of the late Percy Bingham, founder of the Bingham Department Store chain, was robbed at gunpoint by a would-be burglar.

Friday the thirteenth turned out to be an unlucky day for the lifelong Cleveland resident as she was awakened by a loud noise while she slept in the south wing of the mansion usually used by guests.

According to police reports, the main portion of the mansion was under renovation.

Mrs. Bingham, now in her 80s, told investigators she was startled when the intruder flipped on a light in a seldom used bedroom in the guest quarters. She reported she remained quiet while he rummaged through a dresser apparently unaware that anyone was in the room. When she sat up and was discovered, the intruder held a handgun to her head and whispered, "Lie down and be quiet or you're a dead woman." She told police she was too frightened to do otherwise.

According to police reports, the intruder was described as a clean-shaven white male in his late thirties or early forties, over six-feet tall, weighing about one hundred and eighty pounds and wearing a Cleveland Indians baseball cap, dark clothes and gloves. She said it was obvious he was disguising his voice. Asked if she had ever seen the intruder before, she told the authorities no. The only thing Mrs. Bingham was sure the intruder took was three silver dollars and maybe some currency.

When interviewed by the Bugle, *Detective Lloyd Reynolds of the Cleveland Police Department said they planned to present Mrs. Bingham with a photographic lineup to see if she could identify the perpetrator. In an official statement, Reynolds said he wasn't sure the break-in was related to the other break-ins currently under investigation. He declined to comment further saying that he did not want to compromise the investigation.*

Leland sets the article aside and says, "Apparently the intruder was about your size and build and was wearing a Cleveland Indians baseball cap." He peers over his glasses at me. "Bet the cap was the first thing the detectives asked to see."

"How'd you know?" It's obvious to me that this isn't his first rodeo.

Leland goes to his desk, reaches into the bottom drawer and pulls out a Cleveland Indians baseball cap. He also pulls out a baseball signed by the players. "I'm also an avid baseball fan," he says. "Played college baseball through my sophomore year of college. However, it was too tame for me. Best I keep the cap under wraps or I may also become a suspect."

I find myself bonding with Leland. He puts his pants on one leg at a time—just like the rest of us.

"Did they confiscate the cap?"

"No, they just asked me if I had one."

"Did they confiscate anything?"

"They took photographs of some old silver dollars my father had given me and the Glock 17 I keep in my desk drawer that my father had also given me. It appears Mrs. Bingham had reported the gun pointed at her was a black handgun and that the robber took some silver dollars that had belonged to her late husband."

"I'm impressed," Leland says. "Not too many of my clients understand the difference between burglary and robbery."

"I understand robbery is face to face contact and burglary is where someone breaks into your home or business and steals items that don't belong to them."

"Exactly. That's why the perpetrator of the Bingham break-in could be charged with both," Leland replies, "as well as theft. The felony assault is really a lesser included offense of aggravated robbery. That's why I'd argue that it should not be charged if I were to represent you. Otherwise, you, in essence, would be charged, convicted and punished twice for the same offense—a violation of the double jeopardy provision of the Fifth Amendment to the United States Constitution."

"Are they all felonies?"

"All except theft depending on the value of what was taken. Doesn't sound like the would-be burglar took much—at least not enough to make it a felony."

"They want me to take a polygraph. I said I would since I didn't have anything to hide."

"That's something I advise my clients not to do unless we use a private polygrapher." Leland removes his glasses and pinches the bridge of his nose with his thumb and forefinger. "Even then, someone accused of something he or she didn't do may show what is called deception and thus be deemed to have flunked the polygraph. Besides, the results are not admissible in court." After a pause, Leland asks, "Did they advise you of your rights?"

"Ultimately, they did. That was when I couldn't provide an alibi."

"Your wife—?"

"Carissa and the kids were in Akron visiting Carissa's sister and her family on the night of the break-in. I had had a pretty trying day at the clinic and went to bed early that evening and never left the house."

"We might think about a private polygraph and submit the results," Leland says and scratches his head. "With the Bingham mansion only a few miles away and you without an alibi and you having been identified by Mrs. Bingham as the perpetrator, you have an uphill battle."

I wince. "Am I dead in the water?"

"Until the investigation is complete and I've had time to review the reports and conduct an investigation of my own, I wouldn't be able to tell. Let's just hope Mrs. Bingham doesn't identify you in the live lineup."

"Do I have to participate in the live lineup or can I tell them hell no?"

"Unfortunately, the Fifth Amendment doesn't protect you. It is called non-testimonial evidence and lineups, like fingerprints and handwriting exemplars, can be obtained even over your objection. If you don't willingly submit, the prosecuting attorney can get a court order requiring you to do so."

I slump in my chair as bit by bit my hopes begin to dwindle. "Sounds like I'm between a rock and a hard spot."

"To be upfront and honest with you, in a sense you are. Without a sound alibi to counter the identification, there is cause to worry. However, I have faith in our system of justice and our office would do everything we could, within the bounds of the law, to see that you were not unjustly convicted."

"Does that mean you're willing to take my case?"

"Absolutely. Representing the innocent is my job."

"As I said to the detectives when I was being interviewed, you haven't asked me if I did it."

"It doesn't appear you had the motive. By doing what you've been suspected of doing would be like a dancer cutting off his or her legs or a pianist cutting off his or her fingers. It just ain't gonna happen!"

Even though I'm sure the guilty would not admit it, I'm still perplexed no one has asked me. "For the record, I didn't and even if I was destitute, which I'm not, I wouldn't."

"I know that. And speaking of destitute, you can either pay our usual retainer in a case like this or pay as you go. Your call!"

"What would the usual retainer be?"

"Twenty-five thousand dollars."

I'm not surprised. That's less than I expected. I had transferred funds from savings into checking anticipating writing a check so I have enough in checking to cover the retainer. "I'll leave a check with Brenda."

"She'll have a receipt and engagement letter waiting."

"The physical lineup is tentatively scheduled for Wednesday. Will you be there with me?"

"If it's in the afternoon, I will. Otherwise, I'll arrange for another lawyer in the firm to be present. I'd prefer to be there to make sure it's not unduly suggestive. The lineup will already have been tainted by the photographic lineup—which, incidentally, we have yet to review. That may be our whole case."

WHEN WE ARRIVE AT the CPD we are immediately ushered into Reynold's office. The look on his face tells me that he is not at all pleased to see me with an attorney. "So our paths cross again," Reynolds says to Leland, as the two shake hands. Reynolds turns to me, "Dr. Rudland," he says and extends his hand. "Sorry to cause you all the trouble. Detective Summers is in meeting with Mrs. Bingham. We're still rounding up the other seven who will be appearing in the lineup." This is one of the few times being referred to as Dr. Rudland is cause for concern.

Leland is standing beside me and I feel him stiffen as he asks, "Are there some in the physical lineup who were not in the photographic lineup?"

Reynolds looks down and shuffles some papers around on his desk, "Unfortunately, the photographic lineup was put together in a rush. That's why we included the newspaper photo of Dr. Rudland. Dr. Rudland is the only one who will appear in both lineups."

Leland folds his arms across his chest and I hear anger tint his words when he says, "I hate to be a party pooper, but we would object to a physical lineup that singles out Dr. Rudland. It's a foregone conclusion Mrs. Bingham will identify him as the perpetrator in light of the fact that she has already picked him out of the photographic lineup."

"We don't have a choice," Reynolds replies. "We have not been able to locate the other seven. Their photographs appeared in our data base and they fit the description of the man who held Mrs. Bingham at gunpoint."

"Strange, none of the men in the photographic lineup have Cleveland Indian baseball caps. Your reports indicate the perpetrator wore one during his encounter with Mrs. Bingham.

That lineup was tainted and the same will be true of this one," Leland says.

"That's what a suppression hearing is all about. Tell it to the judge. We're stuck with what we've got," Reynolds says, and shoots Leland an icy glare.

"Not necessarily," Leland says. "If there is a lineup, we would suggest the lesser of evils would be one with all the participants wearing Cleveland Indian baseball caps. Keep in mind we are still objecting to a lineup that includes only one of the participants that appeared in the photographic lineup—and that is Dr. Rudland."

"Understood," Reynolds says and leaves the room we presume in order to talk with his supervisor.

I'M THE TALLEST OF the participants and the only one who doesn't look like he lives on the street. All of us are wearing Cleveland Indians baseball caps. I suspect the delay was finding eight Cleveland Indians baseball caps. Score one for the good guys. We are asked to stand facing the two-way mirror behind which Mrs. Bingham is viewing the lineup. After a few moments, we're instructed to turn left and then right. After we present the rear view, we are asked to repeat the process. We are not asked to speak.

After the live lineup, I leave the stage and Reynolds is waiting in the hall. He ushers me into a conference room where Leland is waiting. It seems like an eternity before Reynolds returns. "You have again been identified as the perpetrator," Reynolds says, and I detect a slight smirk form on his lips.

CHAPTER 6

THE INDICTMENT

It was a foregone conclusion that Mrs. Bingham would identify me. By the time of the physical lineup she obviously had the picture of the perceived perpetrator imprinted in her mind. Since I was the only one to appear in both lineups, I obviously was the likely choice. So much for the reliability of the eyewitness.

When we arrive back at Leland's office, he immediately makes a call. Forty-five minutes later I'm in Austin Guthrie's office taking a polygraph examination. The machine reminds me of the echocardiogram that we use in our clinic to detect heart disease through the use of sound waves which we trace on a graph.

"Although there are more modern devices than the one Guthrie uses," Leland says, "his results seem to be the most accurate."

After Guthrie asks me a series of what he calls control questions, he asks me three simple questions: Have you ever been in the home of Harriett Porter-Bingham? Did you break into the home of Harriett Porter-Bingham on October thirteenth, two-thousand and seventeen? Did you leave your home at any time on the evening or night of October thirteenth, two-thousand and seventeen? To all three I answer "No."

When I ask how I did, Guthrie says, "We're not through yet. We need to verify the results," and he administers a second test. When he's through he gathers up his graphs, and excusing himself heads for an adjacent room. I'm in the waiting room with Leland when he emerges. "No deception detected," he says and smiles.

"Does that mean I passed?" I ask.

"Indeed it does, lad," Austin says.

I'm so relieved I sag in my chair and almost cry. *Thank you, God.*

Leland shakes my hand and slaps me on the back.

"First good news in this chapter of my life," I say.

"Hopefully it's only the beginning," Leland says as we head for the parking garage.

As we drive away, I can't help but wonder how this helps my case. "Do the results help my case?"

"Although polygraph results are inadmissible in court, it does help with our negotiations and gives us at least a psychological advantage. Even though it's a lost cause, I will try to get the results admitted into evidence. It can't hurt to let the presiding judge know you're innocent."

"When you say negotiations, does that mean there's a chance the prosecuting attorney may decline filing charges?"

"Depends on how much flack he receives from the CPD. Reynolds seems hell-bent on solving the break-ins and this one in particular. His department has been receiving a lot of bad press lately and I'm sure the CPD has been receiving a lot of pressure from the city council."

"So, I'm the whipping boy."

"Appears so."

I shake my head, as I go from being up-beat back to feeling beat-up. "Wonder how much pressure is being applied by Mrs. Bingham?"

"She's head-strong and may figure it's now her credibility versus yours. A dismissal would mean she's made a mistake, which I doubt she would readily admit."

"Even if it means an innocent man may be convicted?" I shudder at the prospect.

"Even then!"

WHEN I ARRIVE HOME, I pull Carissa aside and ask, "Do you want to hear the good news or the bad news first?"

Carissa hesitates for a moment. "The bad news," she finally says and cringes.

"Mrs. Bingham picked me out of the physical lineup."

"Oh, my God!" Carissa says, and buries her head in her hands. "That's not something I expected. How could she—?"

"She had already picked me out of the photographic lineup and I'm the only one from the photographic lineup who appeared in the physical lineup. How could she not pick me?"

"Is that even fair?"

"Leland says the second lineup was tainted by the first and the first was tainted by what he called an unduly suggestive lineup. Apparently, I was the only one that was not dressed in jail garb, among other things, and… I was the only one that was clean shaven."

"Please tell me this isn't happening," Carissa sobs.

I pull her into my arms. "Leland says we have a chance to get the identification thrown out, and unless there was some evidence left at the scene pointing in my direction, the prosecution doesn't have a case."

Carissa breaks free from my embrace and pushes me away from her. "Oh, my God, does that mean we're going to court and all this will be splashed in the newspapers?"

I jam my hands into my pants pockets and stroll to the window. Autumn is my favorite time of year. However, this year I barely noticed that the trees had turned. Looking back at Carissa, I say, "Not if Leland can prove to the prosecuting attorney that they don't have a case and that if they pursue it, it will be thrown out."

Carissa stubbornly stands her ground. "And how likely is that?"

Carissa's callous attitude surprises me. I thought she'd be more understanding. Now I find I have to defend myself at home, as well as in the courts. Hoping to soften her stance, I say, "Fairly likely."

"Sure. I'll believe it when I see it…"

If I had the energy, this encounter could escalate into an ugly confrontation. I choose to pass and say, "Besides, you didn't ask about the good news."

"Dare I ask?"

I ignore the sarcasm. "I passed the polygraph!"

Looking surprised, Carissa asks, "When did you take a polygraph?"

"Shortly after the physical lineup."

"I thought you said polygraph results were not admissible in court."

"They're not."

"Then why…? If it can't be used to benefit you, how does passing it translate into good news?"

"Leland says we can use it as a bargaining chip. Armed with the polygraph results and the fact that the identification is suspect, he thinks he can convince the prosecuting attorney not to file charges."

Carissa shakes her head. "That's a lot of supposition and does little to reassure us, or at least, me. I don't even know who the prosecuting attorney is. Maybe he'll be persuaded by the pressure exerted on him by the Binghams and their money—"

I interrupt Carissa, hoping to head off a tirade. "Russell Dawson is the elected prosecutor. He is a handball buddy of Leland's. Leland says Russell's his own man."

"Come on, Monty. Don't you know they're all in it together? Dawson's not going to buck the establishment or do anything to offend the high and mighty Binghams and their clique or even the cops. Why should he put his career on the line to appease you? The public is already pressuring the cops to get an arrest in the burglary cases. Get real, you're the sacrificial lamb."

Carissa's words cut me to the quick, and I'm feeling like an island in a sea of misery. I blurt, "Don't you turn on me, too! Don't the polygraph results mean anything?"

"Honey, I'm not turning on you. I'm just frustrated and disappointed in the system, not you. I know you didn't do it! I can't believe this is happening to us. It all seems like a bad dream."

Neither of us can hold back the tears. "We can get through this," I say, as much to reassure myself as her. "Best we not say anything to anyone until we know for sure."

Carissa nods. "Especially not to my parents or the children."

"And not to my parents or even my sister," I say.

"How about the doctors in your clinic?"

I flinch. "Especially not to them. At least not until we're sure charges will be filed. Leland said he's friends with Dawson and will be playing handball with him later in the week. He said he would call him first thing tomorrow and elicit a promise from him not to file charges until the two have spoken."

"Won't the polygraph results prove you're innocent?"

"Not sure what weight that will carry with Russell since polygraph results are not admissible in court. Apparently, the polygraph is not that reliable."

"So we're back to square one and the supposed 'good news' is actually not worth a tinker's damn in the whole scheme of things. What a crazy system. Just out of the blue someone can accuse you of something, someone you don't even know, and turn your whole life and everyone's life around you upside down."

I'm having trouble keeping myself buoyed, much less trying to throw Carissa a lifeline. "Appears so. Guess we have to believe in the system, as flawed as it is," is all I can manage to say.

"Too bad I happened to be at Amber's that weekend. Otherwise, I could have vouched that you were here with your family the whole time."

I realize her world is crumbling along with mine. I take her hand and she entwines our fingers. I hope that gesture is a sign of solidarity. "It's not your fault anymore than it's the clinic's fault for placing the ad in the newspaper with my photograph. But for the photograph and the police using it in their lineup as a filler, I wouldn't be in this pickle."

"Reminds me of something Jennifer was reading just the other day in one of her history books. It was something Benjamin Franklin said:

> *For want of a nail the shoe was lost,*
> *For want of a shoe the horse was lost,*
> *For want of a horse the rider was lost,*
> *For want of a rider the battle was lost,*
> *For want of a battle the kingdom was lost,*
> *All for the want of a nail.*

Doesn't that say it all?"

SEVERAL DAYS HAVE PASSED since I've heard from Leland. I'm nervous fearing I could be arrested any moment. Between patients, I retrieve a message from Carissa. "Call me as soon as you are able."

Now what? A myriad of possible catastrophes race through my head as I dial my home number. Carissa answers on the first ring. "Thank goodness for caller ID. I've carefully screened incoming calls picking up only on those names and numbers I recognize."

My pause slows down when I realize Carissa's call isn't an emergency. "Good idea. I just got your message. What's up?"

"Had a call from Leland's secretary. Leland would like to schedule an appointment with you for Saturday morning sometime around nine. Said to tell you everything was on hold for the time being."

"Sounds encouraging." I say, and attempt to disguise my anxiety by adding, "At least it won't ruin our dinner plans for tonight." *Wonder what progress Leland made with Dawson?*

SATURDAY, WHEN I MEET with Leland, he has an even larger stack of investigative reports which have now been placed in a three-ring binder. He also has an identical binder which he hands me. "Yours," he says.

As I start through the various police reports and witness' statements, Leland says, "Study those later. I'll also be going over them with a fine-tooth comb. Suspect the only incriminating thing they have against you is Harriett Bingham's positive ID. Appears since the intruder wore gloves, fingerprints will not be a factor. However, when I met with Russell this morning he said he would still like your fingerprints along with your Glock 17 and silver dollars. He's familiar with your case and says he's already instructed his staff to keep everything under wraps until charges have been filed."

My heart stops. "Until charges have been filed? Does that mean I'm positively going to be arrested and charged?"

"Oh, no. Sorry I upset you. That means until the decision is made whether to file charges or not. Apparently, the chief of police has instructed everyone at the CPD to do the same. Russell promised me that if he makes the decision to charge you, he will give me the heads up and an opportunity to have you turn yourself in."

The words 'opportunity to turn yourself in' sear into my brain. I'm desperately clinging to what little hope I have left when I ask, "Did you give him a copy of my polygraph results?"

"I did and lobbied in your behalf. He had already confirmed you had no criminal record. Copies of the NCIC and OCIC reports will no doubt be included in the materials we have been provided."

"Does any of that count?"

"Whether that will result in no charges being filed is something not even he knows. He said both your clean record and the polygraph results would work in your favor in the setting of bond should it come to that."

I want to circumvent all the legal mumble-jumble so I ask a direct question. "What are my chances that charges won't be filed?"

"Russell said he's under pressure from all sides to file charges. Apparently the CPD is convinced you're the perpetrator. He also said that the press has been hounding him on the basis of a tip they received from an anonymous source that a celebrity had been arrested in the Bingham robbery and presumably the unsolved burglaries."

Celebrity? That's rich. How'd I go from family doctor to celebrity—just like everything else in this debacle. I go from owning a baseball cap to being a burglar and robber. "Oh, my God!

Now I'm not only implicated in the Bingham robbery, but all the unsolved crimes that ever happened in the past one-hundred years."

Leland smiles. "Still have a sense of humor, I see. Although he didn't say, I'm sure he's been receiving daily calls from Harriett Bingham's family attorney wondering what the delay is in filing charges."

"Sounds like Harriett Bingham is pulling the strings and is not only the accuser, but judge, jury and executioner—all rolled up into one."

"She does wield a lot of power around here, I must admit. The family enterprises generate a lot of paychecks locally. But take heart. There's nothing to corroborate the ID—other than the Cleveland Indian's baseball cap, something every baseball fan in these parts can lay claim to. And the handgun, I doubt the judge would admit. The same thing is true of the silver dollars."

My brain refuses to once again accept that there may be a way out of this for me. "Don't count on it," I say. "I'm sure she will have the judge in her hip pocket along with everyone else."

WHEN I ARRIVE HOME, I go to my den. With all that's happened, even home doesn't feel like a sanctuary. I'm spinning trying to cope with my crisis and I don't see Carissa enter.

"I'm feeling like a widow," she says as she plops down on the leather couch beside me. She glances at the notebook Leland gave me and says, "Trying to find out where the hipbone is attached?"

"Naw, just reading the police reports Leland gave me this morning."

"Let me see," she says and snuggles up next to me.

I slide the notebook in her direction and flip to the interview of Harriett Bingham. After a few pages we read:

"Could you identify the man who robbed you if you saw him again"?

"Absolutely. Never had a gun poked in my face before. We were eyeball to eyeball. I could never forget that face. There was evil in his eyes and I knew I'd better not cross him."

"What color eyes did he have?"

"Dark brown that blended in with his complexion."

"Did he have any facial hair?"

"Just a stubble."

I drop my chin. Before I can say anything, Carissa says, "I thought they said you matched the description. You have blue eyes and anything but a dark complexion."

"They also claim she said the intruder was clean shaven. They must not read their own reports."

"So much for their impartial lineup!"

Dare I hope? "Good catch, Carissa. Hope Leland picked up on the discrepancies."

"As precise as he is, I'm sure he will. I think you should call him just to be sure. We can't afford to leave anything up to chance!"

"He's not in town. He mentioned something about heading to the mountains with his family as soon as he finished with me."

"Bethany said the same thing. My memory isn't what it used to be. Guess I've too much on my mind," she says and shakes her head.

"We all do. I'll call Leland first thing Monday. In fact, he said after I had finished reading the reports to call him."

When Carissa and I finish reading the reports, we're astounded at the lack of evidence they've gathered.

"It's obvious you're the target," Carissa says. "The evidence they have they could put in a thimble. The only evidence they have that there was even a break-in is Harriett Bingham's say so. Don't you find it rather odd that with all the valuables in the mansion the only thing the would-be burglar took was a handful of silver dollars and maybe some currency although it doesn't say how much?"

I think about Carissa's comment for a moment. "Why would someone like Harriett Bingham make up such a story?"

"To get attention, no doubt. I haven't seen her name in the papers recently, and she's used to a lot of press."

"Not used to sleeping in the guest wing of the mansion and being all alone might have caused her imagination to run wild. Even the police reports indicate there was no evidence of forced entry."

"Maybe it was the ghost of her late husband, Percy Bingham, who is said to walk the halls at night that she saw."

A small smile forms on Carissa's lips and she elbows me in the ribs. "Was he a tall, blue-eyed, good looking hunk?"

I squeeze Carissa's hand, acknowledging her tease. "She said brown eyes. Wonder what color eyes Percy had, and if he was clean shaven or had a stubble."

LELAND BEATS ME TO the punch on Monday. "Sorry to call you at home. Hope it's not too early."

I look at the clock. Five-thirty. "Ah, no, I say." Before I can get my wits about me, Leland says, "Did you get a chance to read the police reports?"

"Rubbing sleep from my eyes, I say, "Yes—."

"Did you notice the description of the so-called robber Harriett Bingham gave the police right after the incident?"

Once again I feel a glimmer of hope. "I did! Doesn't match yours truly or the description the detectives told me she gave them."

"Just thought I'd call and give you something positive to think about today," Leland says and hangs up.

WHEN I MEET WITH Leland on Wednesday he tells me Russell is going to present the case to the grand jury when they meet the following evening.

"What does that mean?" I ask.

"It means Russell will present your case to a panel of twelve citizens who will make the charging decision instead of him. Grand juries are a common way to leave the charging decision in sensitive cases to citizens picked by the chief judge. Only the prosecuting attorney presents evidence although the accused usually has the opportunity to testify. Sometimes the accused is subpoenaed and sometimes not. Usually, the accused invokes his or her Fifth Amendment rights against self-incrimination."

"Why a grand jury in my case?"

"I asked Russell the same question. He said he's caught between a rock and a hard spot. He said whatever decision he makes he will be accused of political favoritism. Although I pointed out the weaknesses in his case, he said it really boils down to who to believe. He said he will raise the flag and see who salutes."

"Will you be there to see that I'm not railroaded and will I be testifying?"

"I will only be allowed to be present if and when you testify. I will be precluded from objecting or participating except to be there if you need to confer with me. In answer to your second question, we'll need to discuss that."

"What do I have to lose?"

"The only downside is that anything you say before the grand jury can be used at trial to impeach you if you testify at trial. If you don't testify before the grand jury it's likely they'll indict you."

Dammed if I do and dammed if I don't. "Will Harriett Bingham be testifying?"

"I think that's the main reason Russell is calling a grand jury. Right now, it's your word against hers and hers is suspect in light of the polygraph results. Her inconsistent description of you and the lack of any corroborating evidence may also come into play. If you testify before the grand jury, I think you have a real chance. Too bad you don't have an alibi witness then I would say there would be very little chance of an indictment."

"If they don't indict me, can I still be prosecuted?"

"Theoretically, yes. However, that's not the usual case. In fact, I've never heard of that ever happening."

With my luck… "All I can tell them is I didn't do it."

"There is that! That's a quandary those accused of a crime often face. How do you prove a negative—especially without an alibi witness?"

"Are you telling me not to get my hopes up?"

"To be totally honest and up-front with you, after you testify you didn't do it, all you can do is pray!"

Hell, my knees are already worn to the bone from the praying. I could have received this same advice from Fr. O'Brian without having to pay for it and saved myself twenty-five grand.

THURSDAY NIGHT I'LL REMEMBER in more ways than one. November second is Paxton's birthday and my introduction to the criminal justice system up close and personal. As I wait outside the grand jury room with Leland, I encounter Summers. He seems friendly enough and we exchange nods. Shortly thereafter Reynolds emerges from the grand jury room accompanied by who I later learned was the special investigator for the grand jury. Summers and Reynolds depart and Leland and I are ushered into the grand jury room.

After I take the oath to tell the truth and keep confidential what transpires before the grand jury, I'm asked a series of questions Russell reads from a script.

"State your full name and address."

"Dr. Montel Rudland, twenty forty-six Burnt Mill Road, Shaker Heights, Ohio."

"What is your main profession or occupation?"

"I'm a medical doctor associated with the Talman Medical Center here in Cleveland."

"Dr. Rudland, are you familiar with a person by the name of Harriett Porter-Bingham?"

"Only by name and what I read in the newspaper."

"Are you familiar with what's called the Bingham Mansion on McCallum Boulevard located only a few miles from your home?"

"My family and I ride our bicycles by there on occasion. However, I've never been inside."

"On Friday, October thirteenth, twenty-seventeen, were you in the vicinity of Bingham Mansion?"

Here it comes. I shift my weight in the witness chair. "No, I was at home the whole evening."

"Never left home during that time?"

"No."

"Do you own a Cleveland Indians baseball cap?"

"Yes, wear it to the games."

"Were you at a game that night?"

"No."

"Own a handgun?"

"Yes, a Glock 17 that I keep in my desk drawer at home."

"Is it dark in color?"

"Yes."

"Own any silver dollars minted in the 1890s?"

"Yes, they were given to me by my father."

"Did you enter the Bingham Mansion on Friday, October 13, 2017?"

"No."

"Did you hold a gun on Mrs. Bingham and take any 1890 silver dollars from her?"

"No."

"If Mrs. Bingham identified you as the man who robbed her at gunpoint, would she be mistaken?

"Absolutely."

"Did you try to disguise your appearance on the night in question by using shoe polish or other substance?"

"No."

"Do you have an alibi for the time Mrs. Bingham was robbed by an armed intruder?"

"No. Only my word. My wife and kids were out of town at that time."

"Did you take a polygraph and pass it?"

"Yes."

Russell pauses, and then looking in the direction of the grand jury asks, "Do any members of the grand jury have any questions of Dr. Rudland?"

One of the grand jurors raises his hand. "Dr. Rudland, how tall are you?"

"About six three."

"How much do you weigh?"

"About one eighty-five to one ninety."

"Do you wear contacts?"

"No, I have 20-20 vision in both eyes."

"Thank you."

I'M RELIEVED TO HAVE that behind me, and in fact, surprised how simple it was. On the way to the car, I tell Leland, "I can't believe how impartial the prosecuting attorney was. He seemed to bend over backwards to present the facts as they were and not slant them in favor of one side or the other."

"That's what prosecuting attorneys are supposed to do," Leland responds. "Unfortunately there are some who think their job is to convict, not seek justice. With Russell, you usually get a clean shake."

"I get the feeling he's not entirely convinced I'm the perpetrator."

"He doesn't want to go to trial on a weak case and lose. It only takes losing one high profile case to label him as a loser. Certainly, if and when your case hits the news outlets, he'll be under extreme public scrutiny. As I said before, it's a no-win situation for him. If he gets a conviction, there will be those who are outraged and if he doesn't there will be just as many who are outraged. After all, he has to run for office every four years."

When Leland says high profile case I cringe. I thought the definition of high profile involved someone who was well known to the public at large and generated a lot of attention, like O.J. did in the Simpson murder prosecution. I guess Bingham's social position, and my medical profession make this simple robbery a high profile case. Or, maybe it's my notoriety as a football star in the mold of an O.J. Or maybe it's all the unsolved burglaries.

"If I'm hearing you right, the grand jury is the prosecuting attorney's sounding board."

"You might say that. It is also a way to shift the blame in the event the grand jury declines to indict. With Russell, I think he wants to do the right thing. Knowing him as well as I do, I really think that's the case. Presenting the polygraph results, which are not admissible at trial, is but one example. It would be interesting to see how often that happens."

I'm still stinging from being questioned by a layperson, so I ask, "Why the third degree from the grand juror?"

"It's obvious Mrs. Bingham has already testified and described the perpetrator. Also, Summers and Reynolds no doubt testified as to the description given them by Mrs. Bingham. Knowing Russell, he'll want to cover all the bases. After all, his case hinges on eyewitness testimony and what better way than to call the eyewitness herself."

THE WEEKEND PASSES AND no news from the grand jury. On Monday, between patients, I get a call from Leland. My heart begins to race. He wouldn't call if it weren't extremely important.

"Hello."

"Monty, I received a telephone call from Russell. He said the grand jury would be returning a true bill."

In that instant, my last glimmer of hope dwindles. "Does that mean what I think it means?"

"They will be presenting it before the chief judge sometime this week. The indictment is for three felonies, aggravated burglary, aggravated robbery and felony assault. Not what we expected in light of all the exculpatory evidence and lack of circumstantial evidence to corroborate the eyewitness account."

I'm stunned and feel like I've been punched in the gut. I really don't know what to say or where to start. I finally say, "I'm booked until three. Can you squeeze me in after that?"

"Make it four. That will give me time to rearrange my schedule."

"Okay," is all I can say.

All kinds of things race through my head. *Don't panic, count to ten.* I opt not to tell Carissa until after I meet with Leland.

"MR. WINTHROP IS WAITING for you," the receptionist says and leads me to Leland's office. Leland greets me and points to the familiar chairs which are once again positioned to face each other.

"Grab a seat," Leland says and gestures to my usual place. "Everything is not as bleak as it seems."

"How much bleaker could it be?" I slump in the chair and refrain from making eye contact. I refuse to reignite that glimmer of hope. After a long silence, I say, "Guess I can kiss my family, career and practice goodbye. The medical board and the media will have a hay day with this. Hope the county hotel has a jumpsuit in my size." It finally sinks in when I say it out loud and I want to scream and throw things. I have to fight to control the emotion that overwhelms me.

When Leland doesn't respond, I say, "I can't believe the grand jury would indict. How the hell can they believe the testimony of a senile old lady who needs a nurse to wipe her ass? I don't even fit the description of the perpetrator, if indeed there ever was one…"

In the middle of my tirade, Leland's phone rings. He holds up a finger indicating for me to hold on a minute. Rounding his desk, he answers it. "It's quite alright, Stephanie. What is it?

...tell him I'll call him right back. He's on break and calling on his cellphone from the courthouse? ...okay, never mind, put the call through." Leland covers the mouthpiece and whispers, "It's Russell." Back on the phone, he says, "He's in my office as we speak... no it's not your fault... Can we wait until Wednesday afternoon? ... I appreciate that... Can you stave off the media blitz until then? ... Great... When do you want him to do that? ... That would probably work, I'll ask him... I'll call you first thing tomorrow."

When Leland hangs up, he says, "Russell apologized for the indictment. That's a first. Apparently he's as surprised as we are. He said they would arrange for the foreman of the grand jury to present the true bill in open court on Wednesday afternoon—your afternoon away from the clinic. They, of course, want you present in court. He said they would not oppose a PR bond. That way you won't have to post bail, only promise to appear at all future court appearances."

"Sounds as though the polygraph results and my clean record worked in my favor, at least as far as bond is concerned."

"Absolutely. Those factors will be brought to the attention of the presiding judge who, incidentally, is Chief Judge Ian Grimsley. Grimsley was a former football star at Ohio State and a former law partner of my father. After the court appearance, we will need to stop by the CPD to have you fingerprinted and a mugshot taken. Until then, Russell has agreed to hold up on any press release. Unfortunately, once you appear in court the press will have free reign. Be prepared for the media blitz."

Media blitz! Oh, my God. I shudder when I think of the fallout. "When should I tell Carissa and my associates at Talman Medical Center? As far as I know that may be the end of my marriage and the end of my medical career."

Leland leans forward and pats me on the knee. "I doubt Carissa will abandon you. However, you'll probably be placed on a sabbatical of some sort at the clinic, at least until the dust settles. As far as the Ohio Medical Association is concerned, my experience is they don't do anything until you're found guilty and then only after all the appeals have been exhausted. Since none of this involves any medical malpractice claims I assume you would still be able to practice medicine."

His assumption does little to reassure me. "I've been around long enough to know that, for all intents and purposes, my career is finished even if I'm found not guilty. Once my arrest and prosecution are plastered in every media outlet I will be a pariah—someone no one will want to be affiliated with. I already feel like an outcast."

"Sometimes the mere accusation is as disastrous as a conviction. I guess you'll find out in short order who your true friends are."

"I accept the fact that I'm toast. As you just pointed out, an accusation is as deadly as a conviction as far as my career is concerned. Now I'm more worried about my family. My poor wife and kids. Can't imagine what they're going to go through."

Leland nods. "You need to be upfront with Carissa. She'll no doubt have ideas on how to break the news to Jayden, Jennifer and Paxton."

Then I suddenly remember I haven't told my parents or Carissa's. "My folks won't be happy. And my sister Sandy—I don't even want to think of how she'll react. My in-laws will probably be the toughest to deal with."

RATHER THAN BE SUSPENDED or fired, I turn my resignation into Talman Medical Center. When I explain the circumstances, they're stunned. An impromptu meeting is called for later in the afternoon and they all agree I should be placed on indefinite leave. I'm moved to tears when they persuade me to withdraw my resignation.

On the home front, things are not quite as easy. Although Carissa coaxes me to take heart, I can see in her eyes things have changed. It may be my state of mind, but I sense her loving gestures seem to be forced. Even with my children I detect a sudden change. I'm no longer standing on a pedestal but immersed in mire up to my eyeballs.

CHAPTER 7

THE ARREST

Wednesday, November eighth, is a day that will haunt me forever. It's the day the grand jury returned their indictment in open court charging me with aggravated burglary, aggravated robbery and felony assault—all felonies.

The media apparently were not alerted as to what was in store that unusually warm autumn day. Only those covering the court beat are present and I feel fortunate there are few in attendance. When the foreman of the grand jury presents what Leland calls a true bill signed by the foreman and the prosecuting attorney my heart skips a few beats. Chief Judge Ian Grimsley's stare is as imposing as that of any linebacker I faced. I shudder at the thought of him being my trial judge.

No doubt sensing my discomfort, Leland whispers, "Anyone seen in court with me is presumed to be the baddest of the bad."

If that was supposed to comfort me, it failed miserably.

After Judge Grimsley, a fitting last name I might add, reads the Indictment, he announces, "Because of the nature and severity of the offenses, the court will issue a warrant for the arrest of the named accused." He then signs a document he pulls from a file folder in the lateral file stand on his desk. Studying the paperwork, he asks Russell, "Should I recognize the name Montel Rudland?"

"Your Honor, perhaps you might," Russell says. "Dr. Rudland was an All-American at Iowa some years after your playing days at Ohio State. Also, he is a practicing physician here in Cleveland. In fact, he is present here in court, along with his attorney, to accept the warrant."

Judge Grimsley looks up from filling out the warrant. "What kind of bond is your office requesting?"

"A PR bond, Your Honor."

"A PR bond?"

When the judge questions Russell on the bond, I sink lower in my chair. *What if he doesn't agree to it?*

"Yes, Your Honor. Dr. Rudland's photograph was picked out of a photographic lineup to begin with containing a randomly selected photo of him from a newspaper ad."

"And you presented this case to a grand jury, obviously."

"We did, Your Honor."

"Mr. Winthrop, would you and your client please come forward and position yourselves at the defendant's table."

We do as directed.

"Please be seated a few moments," Judge Grimsley says and motions his clerk to approach the bench. "Here, run copies and give a set to Mr. Winthrop and a set to Dr. Rudland." When she returns, she hands the originals to Judge Grimsley and a set to both Leland and me.

"Dr. Rudland." At Leland's urging, I stand. The judge reads the Indictment and advises me of my rights as well as the penalties in the event of a conviction. "Do you understand the nature of the charges, the penalties and your constitutional rights?"

"I do, Your Honor."

"And how do you plead to the charges?"

"Not guilty, Your Honor."

"Very well, the court will set your bond in the amount of seventy-five thousand dollars. The prosecuting attorney has indicated he doesn't oppose a personal recognizance bond." The judge peers over his glasses and stares down at me from the bench. "Do you know what that is?"

At this point, I refuse to be intimidated. I stand straighter when I answer, "Yes, instead of posting bail my bond is my promise to appear at all court proceedings."

"Well stated! If you fail to appear, your bond will be revoked and you will find yourself in a place you don't want to be. Do you understand that, Dr. Rudland?"

His condescending attitude is insulting. *I'm already in a place I don't want to be and through no fault of my own.* I answer, "Yes, of course, Your Honor."

"Following your court appearance here today, you will need to report to the Cleveland Police Department to be fingerprinted and processed. Good luck, Dr. Rudland."

Good luck! That's a joke. I almost laugh out loud.

Judge Grimsley continues. "Would the attorneys meet with the clerk to set a time for a hearing on any pretrial motions? The parties shall have twenty days from today's date to file motions. If there is nothing further this court will stand adjourned."

Before we even exit the courtroom, we are met by a reporter from the *Cleveland Daily Bugle* who apparently is assigned the courthouse beat. "Does your client have a defense?" the pesky reporter asks and pokes a recorder in Leland's face.

"Yes," Leland responds and quickens his pace with me close behind.

"What is it?" the reporter persists.

Leland stops in his tracks and says, "Case of mistaken identity. The eyewitness has tagged the wrong man."

When the reporter turns her cellphone in my direction, I assume she's photographing me. I instinctively smile hoping the smile will convey my innocence.

By the time we exit the courthouse, we are swarmed by members of the media fighting for access to Leland and myself.

"Who the hell tipped them off?" Leland says. When I look back I see Russell being surrounded by camera crews and microphones being shoved in his face. I almost knock a cameraman down trying to keep pace with Leland. *Sure that shot will delight the viewers.* I can just imagine the headline, "EX-FOOTBALL PLAYER ATTACKS REPORTER."

When we reach Leland's car we make our getaway before the reporters can regroup.

"Whew!" Leland says as he checks to make sure he's all in one piece. "You okay?"

"That was worse than a quarterback sneak," I say worried about the cameraman I almost trampled. "Thanks for running interference."

AT SIX-THIRTY THE FOLLOWING morning, I'm awakened by Carissa who hands me the morning edition of the *Cleveland Daily Bugle*. "Hey, Slugger, looks like you made the front page." The headlines read, *PROMINENT PHYSICIAN INDICTED ON BURGLARY/ROBBERY CHARGES.*

Now I'm wide awake. I grab the paper and sit up. Carissa curls up on the bed beside me. We read:

> *Dr. Montel Rudland, pictured above, has been charged in the burglary and robbery of longtime resident, Harriett Porter-Bingham.*

> *According to police reports, Mrs. Bingham was awakened by a burglar who then robbed her at gunpoint.*

A reliable source said the burglar/robber was identified from a photographic lineup and later by a live or physical lineup.

The description she gave the police of the perpetrator reputedly matched those of Dr. Rudland, a former high school and college football star. "I'll never forget that face," Mrs. Bingham reputedly told authorities, "I've never had a gun pointed at me before."

When asked why he used a grand jury instead of filing direct, prosecuting attorney Russell Dawson told the Cleveland Daily Bugle *there were problems with the case and it was a matter of "he said—she said." He refused to comment further.*

Both sides were given twenty days to file motions and a hearing was scheduled on the motions for Friday, December 1, 2017 at 9:00 a.m. Dr. Rudland's bond was continued to that date.

Mrs. Bingham declined comment when contacted by the Cleveland Daily Bugle.

WHEN NEXT I MEET with Leland, he has five motions ready for me to review. The first is a motion to suppress both lineups. The second is a motion to suppress the use of or any reference to *my* Cleveland Indians baseball cap, the silver dollars found at my home and the Glock 17 handgun. The third is to suppress my statements to the police prior to having been given my Miranda warnings. The fourth is to dismiss the felony assault charge on the grounds that it was the lesser included of the aggravated robbery charge. The last is to allow my polygraph results to be introduced in evidence at trial.

"The first lineup was unduly suggestive," Leland says. "Yours was the only portrait. The other seven were mug shots. Mrs. Bingham had described the perpetrator as clean shaven. The others in the photographic lineup were anything but clean shaven. You were the only one without whiskers. Your photograph stood out like a mole on the end of a beauty queen's nose. Mrs. Bingham said the perpetrator's eyes were brown, yours are blue. Go figure. Some in the lineup had brown eyes, some had blue eyes. The detectives didn't match the participants to the description given by the so-called victim very well."

"What about the physical lineup? Wasn't it just as contrived?"

"Yes, and that's an easy one. The second was tainted by the first. You being the only one in both lineups is a gimme. She already had a vision of you before you even participated in the physical lineup—not from the so-called robbery but from having viewed the unduly suggestive photographic lineup."

"What happens if the court grants our motion and the two lineups are thrown out?"

"Theoretically, the prosecution would have no case. Under the poisonous tree doctrine, if the lineups are tainted then so is the in-court identification. That means Mrs. Bingham would be precluded at trial from identifying you. And without an in-court identification by the so-called eyewitness and without circumstantial evidence such as fingerprints or DNA left at the scene or the fruits of the crime being found at your residence, they have no case."

Hope begins to spring up in my breast. Still seeking confirmation that I could actually win this, I ask, "How about my Cleveland Indians baseball cap, the silver dollars and the Glock 17 handgun?"

"There's no way they can tie them to the crime. How can they show your baseball cap was the same one worn by the would-be burglar, or that the silver dollars were the same ones taken in the burglary/robbery or that your Glock 17 handgun was the same one used by the perpetrator. The point is they can't. All the prosecution can show is that they *look like* the ones involved in the burglary/robbery."

"Wonder how many of the jurors will have similar items. Are they suspects also?"

"If it goes that far, that will be one of our arguments." Leland smiles at me.

"And my statements to the police. Weren't they pretty much benign?"

"There you go talking like a physician again." We both smile this time. "Your statements for the most part were exculpatory and not of an incriminating nature. However, your statements relative to the baseball cap, the silver dollars and the Glock 17 could be considered incriminating in nature. We don't want those items or any reference to those items being introduced in evidence. Also, we'll be arguing that having you produce those items was tantamount to an illegal search. After all, the detectives had no search warrant."

"Sounds as though the prosecution's case crumbles if the court grants our motions to suppress."

"The only one that's iffy is the suppression of your statements. Since you weren't under arrest or in custody, those statements will probably come in."

"Even if I hadn't been read my rights and the statements were made under the guise of having a casual conversation with me?"

"Yes, even then."

"Feels more like entrapment to me."

"Close, but no cigar. Entrapment would be where the detectives caused you to commit a crime that you were not predisposed to commit. Playing good guy/bad guy where one cop appears to be your enemy and the other your friend to lull you into giving incriminating statements is standard operating procedure."

"And the motion to allow the polygraph results?"

"Polygraph results are not scientifically reliable. That one will be summarily denied."

THE COURTROOM IS PACKED when we arrive on that cold snowy December morning. Though we were met by a media welcoming committee when we arrived at the courthouse, the reporters were much more courteous then they were after the Indictment was returned. Not sure what court rules Judge Grimsley had instituted concerning cameras in the courtroom, but before he calls the court to order, the reporters are having a hay day taking pictures with their cellphones.

"Put those away!" Judge Grimsley orders, as he enters the courtroom through his private door. He gathers his robe to him, and positions himself on the platform behind a large oak desk in a high back over-sized executive chair.

After he's satisfied all the participants are present, he asks if either side intends to offer evidence other than what has already been submitted in support and in opposition to the motions. Both Russell and Leland answer no. Turning to Russell, he says, "Mr. Dawson, I assume the prosecution still opposes the motions filed by the defense."

"We do, Your Honor," Russell responds.

"I see you have not filed any motions."

"That is correct, Your Honor. Only the responses to Defendant's motions."

"Mr. Winthrop, the court has read your motions and brief in support thereof as well as the arguments in opposition filed by the prosecuting attorney. Being so informed on your respective contentions and the law applicable thereto, the court makes the following findings and rulings: With respect to suppression of the photographic lineup, the court having reviewed the composite photographs submitted by both sides, does not find the lineup to be unduly suggestive. Therefore, it is a moot question as to whether the physical or live lineup has been tainted. Therefore, Defendant's motion to suppress the victim's identification of the Defendant is hereby denied."

My heart sinks. I think I know how the rest of the trial is going to go.

Judge Grimsley looks up and peers over his glasses at Leland. "I assume you will save an exception."

"We do, Your Honor, and ask that the record reflect our objection," Leland says and shakes his head ever so slightly.

"With reference to the baseball cap, the silver dollars and the Glock 17, the court finds, from the evidence submitted, which is not in conflict, that the items themselves cannot be directly connected to the crimes charged and therefore cannot be admitted in evidence. However, the court will allow the witnesses to refer to those items and the jury can give them whatever weight they desire."

Looking at Russell, Judge Grimsley says, "Mr. Dawson, I see you're champing at the bit. Do you have a problem with the court's ruling?"

"Only clarification, Your Honor. Does that mean that even though Dr. Rudland's baseball cap, for example, can't be introduced in evidence, testimony by the investigating officers concerning having found such a cap at his residence can?"

"According to the evidence submitted by your office, Mr. Dawson," Judge Grimsley responds, "the victim claims the perpetrator wore a Cleveland Indians baseball cap and that a similar, but not necessarily the same cap, was found at Dr. Rudland's residence. After all, thousands of people have a Cleveland Indians baseball cap, including me. That doesn't mean I committed the crime charged."

"Your Honor, we're not arguing about the ruling. We just want to make sure our witnesses can testify as having found a similar cap at Dr. Rudland's residence."

"Yes and the same is true of the other enumerated items found at Dr. Rudland's residence."

"Thank you, Your Honor."

"Any other questions, Mr. Dawson?"

"No, Your Honor."

"Mr. Winthrop?"

"No, Your Honor, not on that issue. I assume you'll be ruling on our motion to eliminate the felony assault charge on the grounds that it is the lesser included charge of aggravated robbery. It's our contention that a defendant cannot be charged, convicted and punished for both aggravated robbery, which requires the use of a deadly weapon in its commission, and felony assault which merely requires the use of a deadly weapon. The felony assault merges into the aggravated robbery."

"The court has read your motion and legal argument in support thereof, Mr. Winthrop, and finds the same to be premature. You can raise it if and when the jury returns a guilty verdict as to both. With regard to your remaining motions, Mr. Winthrop, they will be summarily denied including your motion to admit Dr. Rudland's polygraph results."

"Thank you, Your Honor," Leland says, and I can tell he's not happy with the rulings.

"Very well, the court will set this matter for a one week trial starting sometime after the first of the year. It looks like I'm booked until March. Will that give both sides time to prepare?"

"It will," Russell replies.

"Same for us," Leland replies.

"Mr. Winthrop, I assume you'll be asking for a jury trial."

"We would request a jury of twelve," Leland replies.

"Very well. This matter is set for a jury trial commencing on Monday, March sixth, twenty-eighteen, starting at eight a.m. Dr. Rudland's bond will be continued to that date. If there is nothing further, the court will stand adjourned."

When we leave the courtroom this time Leland avoids the media as we pass without incident.

"I see the cameraman you almost flattened the last time we were in court is staying out of your way," Leland says as we make our way to the parking lot.

"You mess with the bull, you get the horns," I say. I'm upset we didn't succeed in quashing the lineups and am in no mood for humor.

"Win some, lose some," Leland says as we drive away. "For all intents and purposes, all the prosecution has is the flawed eyewitness testimony of Mrs. Bingham."

Somehow that does little to reassure me that everything's going to be all right.

THE NEXT DAY, I retrieve the morning issue of the newspaper. The headlines and article in the *Cleveland Daily Bugle*, along with a photograph of Leland and me leaving the courthouse, read:

ATTEMPT TO STYMIE RUDLAND PROSECUTION FAILS

The prosecution of Cleveland physician Dr. Montel Rudland will proceed to trial as a result of the rulings on Wednesday of Chief Judge Ian Grimsley at a motions hearing wherein the defense sought to quash the eyewitness testimony of heiress Harriett Porter-Bingham.

The ruling validates the lineup where Dr. Rudland was identified as the man who robbed Mrs. Bingham at gunpoint. "The lineup was not unduly suggestive," Judge Grimsley ruled in denying the motion.

Dr. Rudland, a prominent physician, community leader and former high school and college football star, was indicted by a Cuyahoga County grand jury on November 8, 2017. He was charged with aggravated burglary, aggravated robbery and felony assault, all felonies. He pled not guilty to the charges which, if proven, could mean a prison term and a loss of his license to practice medicine in the states of Ohio and Iowa.

A motion to suppress the admission of a Cleveland Indians baseball cap, twenty-three silver dollars and a Glock 17 handgun found at Dr. Rudland's residence was granted because there was no forensic evidence tying the items to the ones connected to the burglary. They could, however, be referred to by the witnesses but not introduced into evidence, Judge Grimsley ruled. Other defense motions, including the admission of polygraph results were also denied.

A trial to a jury of twelve was scheduled for the week of March 6,2018, commencing at 8:00 a.m. Dr. Rudland's bond was continued to that date.

CHAPTER 8
THE DREADED WAIT

I'm like a fish out of water. Between not knowing what my future will bring and having nothing worthwhile to do, I've become a basket case. This morning while we linger over our second cup of coffee, Carissa says, "Monty, you're driving me bats. Since taking the sabbatical all you do is prowl the house. Why don't you go visit your folks for a while? Even if your Dad doesn't need the help, you could sure use the exercise." She points at my paunch.

When Carissa suggests I spend a little time in Hawarden helping my father on the ranch, I jump at the chance.

"Twenty-four days until Christmas," Carissa says. "That's less than a month away. We could spend Christmas there with your family or here at home."

Not wanting to be selfish, I slowly stir my now cold coffee, and ask, "What about your family? Maybe we could split the kids' Christmas vacation between both sets of grandparents."

Carissa perks up. "I like that idea. We could spend the first part of their vacation including Christmas day in Hawarden with your family and the remainder in Des Moines with mine." *That decision was quick. Wonder if that's what she had in mind the whole time.*

With a broad smile, she adds, "The Bundridges are known for their New Year's bashes, you know."

"And how!" I say. "The neighbors called the cops on your brother-in-law and me for shooting pop-bottle rockets on their roof."

"Brandon blamed you and you blamed Brandon when actually it was the Webster's own son Tyler who was the culprit."

Ah, yes, good ole Tyler. "As I recall, Tyler was one of your old boyfriends. Whatever happened to Tyler?"

"The last I heard, he was still in the Air Force and living with his wife and two daughters somewhere in Germany."

"I'm going to have to keep a low profile this year, I'm afraid. One of the conditions of my bond is I not get into any trouble."

"If Tyler is home on leave, we'll make sure he's not invited. As far as Brandon is concerned, you'll have to fend for yourself."

"I'm not sure I'll even be invited. Your parents may consider me an embarrassment."

Carissa snickers. "Mom and Dad aren't like that. Neither is Amber or Brandon. You're still as much a hero to them as you are to me." Carissa reaches across the table and squeezes my hand.

"How do you know?"

"Know what?" Carissa frowns. "Since I've spent a good deal of my life with them, I think I can say with some certainty that my parents are not fair-weather friends, neither is Amber or her family."

"My situation is not one they've faced before. I'm sure I'll be an embarrassment."

"When they know all the facts such as the dubious identification and the fact that you passed a lie detector test, they'll be very understanding."

"They probably already know about the arrest."

"If they do, they haven't said. And I just talked to them yesterday. Fortunately, they've been in Hawaii getting their winter residence ready."

"Let's hope they haven't been watching much TV or following the news."

Carissa changes the subject. "You've got to call your parents. It would be better for you to tell them than for them to hear it from someone else."

I blanch. "That's the part of this whole thing I dread the most—telling those I love that I've been charged with three felonies."

"They'll feel like I did knowing you're not capable of doing such a thing and that there must be some mistake."

"That's what I've always liked about you, Carissa, through thick and thin you've always been there with me."

"I'd be there even if you did it." Carissa stands and gives me a kiss full on the lips as she gathers the cups. "I'll always be here for you."

"HELLO, MONTY, IS THAT you?" Dad says.

"How'd you know?"

"Caller ID. Even though we live in the boonies, we do have some modern technology. Besides you're way overdue. Hold on while I get your mother on the other line."

I can hear Dad yelling, "Willa, Monty's on the phone."

"It's about time," Mom says half scolding as she picks up the extension.

May as well get it over with quick. I say, "I would've called sooner except I'm the bearer of some bad news."

"You needn't ever worry about that," Mom says. "Life is full of setbacks and we hear you've just been dealt some bad cards."

When I don't immediately respond, Dad says, "We already know! Bubba Bolling and his wife, Sylvia, returned several days ago from Cleveland where Sylvia had a hip transplant. They brought with them the newspaper article that was in the *Cleveland Daily Bugle*."

"We wanted to call as soon as we heard, but after some discussion, decided to let you handle this in your own time and in your own way," Mom says.

"I'm sorry!" I murmur. "I've tarnished the Rudland name and am surprised you even want to talk to me."

"Nonsense! You're our son, neither hell nor high water could get us to turn our back on you—not now or ever," Mom replies. "You're part of our prayer chain."

Dad clears his throat, "We've put enough away to hire the best attorney in the state of Ohio. Our attorney here says that Rashard Ginsberg is the attorney he would hire if he were ever in trouble."

"That's nice of you, Dad," I say. "But I already have one of the top criminal law attorneys in the state. He's a Yale graduate by the name of Leland Winthrop. He's a former prosecutor, and as a defense attorney, he has successfully defended a lot of political and sport figures. Many of his cases have appeared in various police magazines."

"As long as you get the best!" Dad prods. "Let me know how much you need and I'll wire it."

"Thanks, Dad. I have enough for now." Feeling ashamed and guilty, I'm amazed no one asks the question so I say, "Aren't you going to ask if I did it?"

"Hell no! Don't have to," Dad says. "Knowing you your whole life through is proof enough that they have the wrong person. Your mother had a dream the night we were told about your arrest that the person who actually committed the crime would be caught. She said it was very vivid and when she's had dreams like that before they were usually true." I hear Mom sniffle in the background.

"Why don't you come spend a few days with us until everything gets sorted out? It would be good for you and besides I could use the help." I'm surprised that Dad doesn't seem to be at all upset with me nor does Mom. If this happened to one of my kids, I'm not sure how I'd feel. Probably the same way.

"Actually, that's why I called. Carissa suggested we split our Christmas vacation between our two families. Carissa, the kids and I would spend the first half including Christmas day with you and the second half including New Year's eve with Carissa's family."

"Could you come and spend time here until the kids are out of school?" Mom asks. "Dad could use the help." I know that's Mom's ploy to get me there. Since Dad injured his hip a couple of years ago, he employs a crew year round to help cover the two thousand five hundred and sixty acres and with Danny overseeing the basic operations, that's all the help they need.

"Carissa has already suggested that," I say. "Can you put up with me for a few weeks?"

"Put up with you! You can stay as long as you want," Dad says.

DANNY MEETS ME AT the Sioux Falls Regional Airport, sixty miles from Hawarden. Danny has put on some weight and when I shake hands, I'm sure it's all muscle. Ranching is a good way to keep in shape. I'm a little taller than Danny and he favors our father and has dark hair and brown eyes. Sandy and I, on the other hand, favor Mom's side of the family. Both of us have blue eyes and light hair.

"We could use an M.D. in Hawarden," Danny says as we wait at the carousel for my luggage. "If they take your license in Ohio, you may still be able to practice in Iowa." It's obvious Danny is familiar with my legal woes. Although both he and his wife, Mildred, are attorneys, they spend more time on the ranch than practicing law. Since they are childless, they don't have to worry about taking kids out of school and are not tied down like Carissa and me.

"I'm anxious to get Mildred's and your take on my case. Not sure I have much faith in the legal system after what's happened to me."

Danny nods. "Say, isn't that your old U of I duffel coming toward us?"

"Sure is," I step forward and grab it from the conveyor belt.

As we leave the parking garage, Danny suggests we stop for lunch in Sioux Falls before heading home. After we order, Danny says, "Even though I'm an attorney, I could be subpoenaed by the prosecution to divulge anything you tell me regarding your case. You and I have no attorney/client privilege."

"But I have nothing to hide. I've never met my accuser, never been in the Bingham Mansion, never held a gun on anyone, never robbed anyone, and have absolutely no criminal record. What if I 'hire' you?"

"Then we have an attorney/client relationship and what you tell me is privileged."

"Okay," I say, and take my wallet from my back pocket. "Here's fifty dollars."

"In that case, lunch is on me." We laugh and over lunch I proceed to tell him about my case—chapter and verse.

"Without seeing the photographs in the photographic lineup, it's obvious your studio photo stood out like a sore thumb. It was unduly suggestive and the photo bore little resemblance to the so-called victim's description of the perpetrator. If the photographic lineup or array was tainted then so is the subsequent physical or police lineup."

I'm impressed by my little brother's grasp of the law and how it applies to my situation. He sounds pretty much like the much older and more seasoned Leland Winthrop. I lean forward to catch every word as Danny continues.

"That means if she attempts to identify you in court, your attorney can object on the grounds that the in-court identification is tainted by the out-of-court identification. Identification is critical in every case. Without Mrs. Bingham's testimony, it doesn't appear the prosecution can tie you to the crimes charged."

"Yeah, we've been down that road. Unfortunately, at the suppression hearing the judge didn't find either lineup to be unduly suggestive."

"Did you see the composite of the lineup, or better yet, did the judge have the composite before him when he made his ruling?"

"It was attached to our motion to suppress as well as the prosecution's response to our motion. So was a photograph of the live lineup."

"I remember a case entitled *Stovall v. Denno*. It was a case handed down by the United States Supreme Court sometime in the mid-1960s. It held it was a violation of an accused's Fourteenth Amendment rights to allow an in-court identification where the accused had previously been subjected to a lineup that was so unnecessarily suggestive that it couldn't help but cause irreparable mistaken identification."

"I think that was one of the cases my attorney cited in his brief."

"I'm sure it was, and I'd be disappointed if it wasn't. That's one of the key cases on in-court identification where the accused had first been identified by a victim prior to trial."

"Can I appeal the ruling prior to trial?"

"Unfortunately, you're going to have to wait until the jury finds you guilty to do so."

I have to walk the plank before I get a life preserver. "That doesn't seem fair!"

"It is what it is. However, that's your ace in the hole. With the scanty evidence you've described, it appears unlikely you'll be found guilty."

Once again I begin to hope. "You really think so?"

"All they have is a Cleveland Indians baseball cap which I assume every baseball fan in Ohio has, some 1890 silver dollars, which by the way Dad also gave Sandy and me, and a handgun that the victim has only described as being black in color. Since those items were held to be inadmissible, the sting I'm sure will be minimal. Even photographs of the items may not be particularly damaging." Danny pauses to take a sip of water, and shaking his head, adds, "I'm surprised the grand jury returned an Indictment."

"Mrs. Bingham's testimony, I'm sure, carried a lot of weight. There were a lot of older people on the jury that idolize the ground she walks on and I'm also sure when it comes down to her word against mine, the community pioneer's word will trump every time over a carpetbagger's, especially a transplant from Iowa."

"That's why you will want a lot of younger people on your trial jury-especially those who have recently migrated from other parts of the country like yourself. Those from middle America with common sense who have to work for a living and weren't born with silver spoons in their mouths are the ones who I'd pick."

ONCE WE'RE BACK ON the road, I ask, "Danny, how is it you and Mildred gave up a lucrative law practice to move to Hawarden where a retainer fee amounts to a couple of chickens and maybe a goat? You've always had a good head on your shoulders and could be raking in the big bucks."

"Ha! You needn't sound so surprised. Don't tell me you haven't accepted a goat or two as payment for setting a broken leg."

"No goats, Carissa prefers the chickens. They're easier to work with." We knuckle bump and share a chuckle.

"But to answer your question, I became disenchanted with the criminal justice system right out of the chute when I first started practice." Danny nods in my direction, "Case in point. It seemed the innocent were found guilty and the guilty given nothing more than a slap on the wrist. Being a prosecutor for a brief period of time was an eye-opener. I like the way nature dispenses its own brand of justice when its laws are broken. Being in control of one's destiny and not dependent on the whims of others is more appealing to me than having to kiss a judge's ass who is on the bench because he can't make a living on his own."

This is a side of Danny I hadn't seen before—and I like it! We exit the highway and take the access road that leads to the ranch. I'm overcome with nostalgia when we approach the gate and I see the name *THE ROYAL FLUSH DOUBLE CIRCLE R RANCH* carved into the redwood arch that is supported by two redwood pillars at the entrance. When I feel tears threaten, I suddenly realize how fragile I've become.

Danny glances my direction, "You okay, bro?"

"Yep!" is all I can manage without completely breaking down.

DAD MEETS US AT the door, and says as he shakes my hand, "The prodigal son returns." Unlike with my own sons, Dad doesn't want an embrace to be misconstrued. Although the reception is warm, it's not like the one Sandy receives when she comes home. Mom, on the other hand, still considers me her little boy and would pick me up and hold me if she could. When I pull out my handkerchief and dab at the tears in her eyes, she exclaims, "Monty, you're skin and bones."

"Won't be after I'm here a week. I've missed you and your cooking."

"Doesn't Carissa ever feed you?" Mom asks, and I sense she's only half joking.

"Yes, Carissa's an excellent cook. It's just that I haven't had much of an appetite lately. Carissa does her best to get me to eat. Guess you might say it's a self-imposed starvation." Mom continues to hold both of my hands in hers when I'm suddenly mauled by Sir Galahad.

"Down, boy!" Dad yells and grabs for Galahad's collar.

Sir Galahad looks more like a wolf than a Siberian Husky and whines when we're separated. Dad lets loose of his collar about the same time Mom lets loose of me. Sir Galahad makes it known he has missed me by licking my hands and wagging his tail. I've lost count of how old he is but in dog years he has to be a couple of hundred years old. Snoopy the cat is also vying for attention. About the size of a poodle and obviously not concerned about her diet, she rubs against my pant legs.

"It's good to have you back home, Monty," Dad says. "Want to see the stallion I won playing horseshoes with Clayton Ritter?"

Dad doesn't seem to be the least bit concerned about my legal woes and he makes me wonder if maybe the past several months have been just a bad dream.

On the way to the stables, I watch as Dad falters and seems to favor his left hip. "Not as agile as I once was," he says. "Maybe its time to turn the ranch over to you and Danny."

I don't want to think that my career as a physician might soon be over, but it's reassuring to know I won't have to go beg on the streets. Ranch life isn't all that easy but it does have its' perks. At least you get plenty of exercise and don't have to take sleeping pills to fall asleep.

To avoid compromising Mom and Dad, Danny suggests he be the one to fill them in on my criminal case. "That way, we don't have to worry about them having to come into court and testify against you," Danny says.

UNFORTUNATELY, OUR PLANS CHANGE when Paxton comes down with the flu. Instead of Carissa and the family flying to Hawarden, it was decided I would just meet them the day after Christmas in Des Moines. Danny and Dad put me through the paces so that by the time I arrive in Des Moines the day following Christmas, I'm in such good condition, I could play in the NFL. When I deplane, I'm met by Carissa and her father. "You look great!" Carissa says and gives me a warm hug.

"And so do you," I say. "I've missed you and the kids."

I shake hands with Carissa's father. If he harbors hostility, I don't detect it.

"Santa left some gifts for you at the house," he says.

We store my luggage and cache of gifts in the trunk and head out of the parking garage. Carissa snuggles close to me and whispers, "Christmas was not the same without you. Even my parents said so. You're the son Dad never had. We missed you terribly."

I struggle to hold back the tears. My self-perceived rejection only exacerbates my guilt. Still, I'm not convinced the Bundridge clan will be all that forgiving if I'm found guilty at trial. I don't want to think what side Carissa would take if I'm considered a blight on her family's good name and a threat to their standing in the community.

When we reach the Bundridge residence, sitting in the driveway is a 2017 white Mercedes with a huge bow holding a large red ribbon together draped around the car.

"Looks like your folks bought themselves a new Mercedes for Christmas," I say to Carissa.

"Tell him, Daddy," Carissa pleads.

"It's a Christmas present from Carissa's mother and me to the two of you," Quinton says. "That will replace the Mazda you've been driving back and forth to the clinic."

"No," I protest, as guilt swarms me. "I don't deserve it especially since I'm on administrative leave from the clinic."

"Call it an early victory present," Quinton says. "Carissa tells me that your trial is in early March and that is only a few months away. From what I've been told about your case, your picture from an ad in the newspaper resulted in your being tagged the burglar."

I don't know what to say. I was dreading having to explain to my family and then to Carissa's family that I had been charged with three felonies. I feel lightheaded and take Carissa's hand in mine. When I look into her eyes, I see her love radiate and I'm once again reinforced. "First Carissa never wavered in her support and belief in my innocence; then my clinic that wouldn't accept my resignation; next were my parents who also expressed their belief in me, and now you. It would have been easy for you to have written me off but you didn't. I…can't thank you enough."

"Say no more. We want to do everything we can to help. The Mercedes is just a start and a pick-me-upper. We have no reason to believe you're involved, and on the contrary, know you're not capable of such a thing." After he parks his car, he hands me a set of keys and says, "Go over and inspect your new ride. It hasn't been moved from that spot since it was delivered."

Carissa walks arm in arm with me to the Mercedes. She gently pulls the big red bow and ribbon from the top of the vehicle and opens the driver's door. The two of us peer inside. When I look at Carissa, she has a big smile on her face. "Surprised?"

"Not just by the car," I respond.

Carissa frowns, but then the smile returns. "Didn't I tell you so?"

Still overwhelmed at the caliber of the gift, I slide onto the driver's seat and grab hold of the steering wheel. I motion with my head for Carissa to join me. She sprints around the front of the car and jumps into the passenger seat.

"Where to, ma'am?" I ask, pretending to pull a cap down lower on my head.

"Hum…Somewhere over the rainbow where dreams really do come true, if you please, sir."

Those damn tears well up again. This time I don't even try to suppress them. "Think there really is such a place?" Carissa slips her hand into mine, as I continue, "Prior to the ordeal, I may have been wrong but never in doubt. Since this nightmare began, I don't know what to believe or who to trust. Around every corner disappointment lurks with an increasingly larger dose of it almost every day."

"Believe and pray as never before," she whispers.

"Don't worry. I've been doing a lot of praying lately. Looks like some of it's working."

QUINTON AND I UNLOAD my luggage and we all go inside. As soon as we enter the house, I'm mobbed by Jayden, Jennifer and Paxton. *God, how I've missed them!* "Daddy, Daddy," Pax yells as he wiggles his way through his older siblings. Even though I haven't been separated from them for very long, Jayden and Jennifer seem taller. *Damn those tears.* I shudder when I think of how much of their lives I'll miss if I'm convicted and sent to prison.

"I haven't been this popular since winning the division title," I say. *A rousing reception I was not expecting. They're the reason I can't just throw in the towel.*

Kayla joins the throng and asks, "How do you like your Christmas present?"

"It's his victory present," Quinton corrects.

"Hey! How about me?" Carissa chimes in.

"Chill, little girl. Your name is on the title too," Quinton replies.

"It's more than generous," I say. "We'd have been happy with a Subaru."

"Speak for yourself," Carissa interjects. "I happen to love it."

Before the situation can get out of hand, Quinton says, "It wasn't as expensive as you think, and it helps to have an interest in a car dealership."

Jennifer has been shifting from foot to foot. It appears she's run out of patience as she says, "You haven't opened your gifts from us."

"And you haven't opened the presents I brought for all of you," I say and look at Carissa. I pull two small jewelry-type boxes from my pocket and hand them to her. Suddenly, everything is moving in slow motion as Carissa opens the gifts. When she extracts a sapphire ring from the first box she squeals with delight. Placing it on her finger, she takes a moment to admire it before tearing into the second box. I hear her sudden intake of breath when she sees the matching sapphire and diamond tennis bracelet displayed on the black velvet interior of the box. Our eyes meet and that moment will be etched in my memory for as long as I live.

"Monty, I don't know what to say," Carissa says, as she holds the tennis bracelet up, dangling it for all to see.

"Do you like it?" I tease.

"Like it, I love it! Here, help me with the clasp." I fumble around for a moment but finally get the job done. "I may never take it off," she exclaims, and she slowly moves the stones around her wrist admiring them one by one.

"I want it," Jennifer says.

"Mine!" Carissa says, and protects her bracelet with her free hand.

AT DINNER, QUINTON ANNOUNCES he and Kayla have had a revelation. "Why don't you consider staying with us until your trial?" He raises his brows and his eyes focus on me.

"Why, I —"

Before I can answer, he says, "Regardless of the outcome, you may or may not want to continue living in the Cleveland area. If you're acquitted, there may be that lingering doubt by those familiar with your case that maybe you did it, and if you're found guilty, you might be required to serve time and Carissa and the kids will need a support group."

"Daddy, he's not going to be found guilty!" Carissa says emphatically.

"You never know," Quinton replies. "We need to be prepared in the event he is."

"We can renovate the guest cottage. You all can stay there," Kayla says. "It needs to be repainted and refurnished anyway."

"What about the kids?" I ask and search their eyes for a reaction.

"They can start the next school term here in Des Moines. We have a great school system here and have everything they have in Cleveland." Quinton looks at Carissa, "That way their schooling wouldn't be disrupted in the event of an adverse verdict."

"And it will save everyone from having to endure the tension the trial and gossip will bring," Kayla says.

"It would make life a lot more tolerable for all of us," Carissa says and looking at me asks, "Honey, what do you think?"

"I hadn't thought about that," I say. "What about our house in Shaker Heights?"

"We could hang onto it until we see what happens, and of course, you and I could stay there during the trial. We don't want the kids being subjected to all the stress, so they could continue to stay here with Mommy and Daddy."

I shake my head.

"Is that a no?" Carissa asks.

Before I can respond, Quinton says, "You could come work at Bundridge Bank and Trust. I need a new loan officer at our main branch. You could be earning a living and at the same time be with your family. It's only until your legal issues are resolved. Who knows, you might like it and open up a medical practice here in Des Moines."

"I can always adjust," I say. "I'm a survivor. However, I worry about Carissa, Jayden, Jennifer and Paxton. If they're happy with such an arrangement, then it's a done deal." All four nod their heads.

"I guess Carissa and I can arrange to have our personal belongings shipped," I say.

"Does that include our computers?" Jayden asks.

"Of course," I say and smile. "How could life even continue without computers?"

Carissa reaches over and kisses me on the cheek. "I love you," she says.

With all the adverse publicity I anticipate a jury trial will generate, I'm grateful for the reprieve. I remember what Leland said about finding out who my true friends are, and I also remember how cruel school kids can be. I want to spare my family as much agony as possible. And at this point, I'm not sure whether I'll be convicted or not.

I'm suddenly full of rage. I try not to reflect on how things were before all this happened. We were living the dream. Our lives were perfect. We had it all. Then, just out of the blue, we lose it all. Quinton hit the nail on the head. Even if I am acquitted, our lives will forever be changed.

CHAPTER 9
THE TRIAL

As I venture into the uncertainty of trial, with all the lopsided events that have beset us up to this point, I don't even dare dream I'll emerge victorious.

Sitting with Leland during jury selection is nerve racking. I study the prospective jurors and wonder how they will view my case. Leland and I previously discussed the kind of juror we thought would weigh the evidence and return a fair verdict, but now, judging from the stern looks on their faces, I'm experiencing doubt that any one of them would. Although we try to get rid of the old liners and ruling class and fill the jury box with newcomers and those we don't think will come under Harriett Bingham's spell, we are stymied by the jury pool. We use up all our challenges on the undesirables and end up with some who are worse than the ones we replace.

"The luck of the draw," Leland says and shrugs. "At least we ended up with seven women."

"And only three of the seven are under thirty," I say.

"Wish we had more middle class jurors—those who had to work hard to make a living."

"Not too many had heard of Harriett Bingham," I say. "At least that's a plus."

"Not any had been victims of a crime." Leland checks his notes. "All the men were gun owners. All but one juror was a coin collector. Four of the five men had Cleveland Indians baseball caps. All read mystery novels. And six said they had been accused sometime in their lives of something they didn't do. That's half the panel, and may work well in our favor."

I nod. "I thought of that as well. The one that bothers me the most is Mrs. Hildebrand who said our system was unfair to those who couldn't afford a high-powdered attorney and looked at me."

"I agree with your assessment of her. If we'd had one more peremptory challenge, I would have used it to oust her. Another one I would have challenged is Mr. McCabe. He'll undoubtedly be the foreman. When asked if the mere charging of a crime meant the accused was guilty, he responded, 'Where there's smoke, there's fire.'"

"I'm surprised Judge Grimsley didn't grant your motion to challenge him for cause. Sounded to me like he already had his mind made up. If that isn't a show of bias, then nothing is. When Russell asked the prospective jurors if any of them had been a patient of mine, the one that raised her hand was immediately excused. Yet those who said they had heard of Harriett Bingham were not." I shake my head in disgust. "I'm more frightened of the judge than I am of the jury."

Leland furrows his brow. "That's been my worry from the start. But then again that's why we have appellate courts."

"Do you really think we'll get that far?" I ask. "Surely as anemic as the evidence is in my case, I can't imagine a jury convicting me—not even this one."

"The trial jury, unlike a grand jury, has to be convinced of your guilt beyond a reasonable doubt. They need more than just an eyewitness account that is unsubstantiated in order to convict, especially where the accused takes the stand and subjects himself or herself to cross-examination.

"As I've stated before, you didn't have a motive. That's why I'm not particularly bothered by Mrs. Hildebrand being on the jury. Besides, what medical doctor would risk his career to take a few silver dollars?"

It took eleven grueling years of college and residency to get my license. Why would I put it on the line for a few silver dollars? Having Leland verbalize what I thought from the beginning was reassuring. "She was the one who said she knew Mrs. Bingham, and I sense she might be jealous of society-types in light of her statement about the privileged. Who knows, maybe as vocal as she is she might be just the type we want on our jury."

Removing his glasses, Leland says, "It will probably boil down to who she resents the most."

"Or the least," I say. We both chuckle.

With the hiatus and my family somewhat removed from the circus-like atmosphere, I'm not surprised that I'm more relaxed in court than I thought I'd be. Although Carissa accompanied me back to Cleveland, Leland strongly suggests she absent herself from the trial. "She doesn't need the stress of being here and you don't need the stress of her being here," he says.

The press swarms over us like bees as we enter and exit the courthouse. The collective petition of several of the television channels to allow cameras in the courtroom was summarily denied by Judge Grimsley. "It would cause a distraction and trials are not spectacles," he had said in making his ruling.

The case of *People of the State of Ohio v. Montel Rudland* again hits the front page of all the newspapers. *You'd think a city the size of Cleveland would have more exciting news to report than a simple burglary/robbery case. Guess because of Bingham's so-*

cial status and me supposedly disgracing the medical profession, it's worthy of front page coverage. The headline and subsequent article in the March eleventh, twenty-eighteen issue of the *Cleveland Daily Bugle* reads:

JURY SELECTED IN HEIRESS ROBBERY CASE

A jury was sworn in late yesterday after the prosecuting and defense attorneys squabbled over who should be empaneled in the prosecution of physician and former football star, Dr. Montel Rudland.

Dr. Rudland was charged in the burglary and robbery of Harriett Porter-Bingham, heir to the Morgan Porter and Bingham Department store fortunes.

According to police reports, Mrs. Bingham was awakened on the night of October 13, 2017, by a would-be burglar. When she startled the intruder, he stuck a handgun in her face and ordered her to lie down and be silent. He then took some silver coins and fled. Mrs. Bingham later identified the intruder as Dr. Montel Rudland, a physician who lived but a few miles away from her Shaker Heights mansion.

Dr. Rudland's attorney, Leland Winthrop, sought unsuccessfully at a hearing on December 1, 2017, to have the photographic and police lineups suppressed because they were "unduly suggestive." He argued that Dr. Rudland's photograph was taken from an ad for his clinic and varied from the description given the police by Mrs. Bingham. He argued to the presiding judge, Ian Grimsley, that the police lineup was tainted by the first lineup and that his client was the only one to appear in both lineups.

In seeking to suppress as evidence a Cleveland Indians baseball cap and twenty-three silver dollars found by police at Dr. Rudland's residence, Winthrop argued there was no evidence to prove the cap was the same one worn by the intruder at the time of the robbery or that the silver dollars found at the Rudland residence were the same ones taken in the robbery. Although the cap and silver dollars will not be allowed in evidence, Judge Grimsley ruled, "They may be referred to by the witnesses."

The trial was recessed until 8:00 a.m. today at which time the prosecution and defense will be making their opening statements followed by the presentation of evidence. When asked by the Cleveland Daily Bugle *how long the trial would last, Prosecuting Attorney Russell Dawson said, "Not more than a week." He refused to comment on how many witnesses he expected to call or what their testimony would be. When asked if Dr. Rudland was involved in any of the other burglaries, he said "Everyone is a suspect at this point."*

RUSSELL, FULL OF CONFIDENCE and looking dapper in his Armani, was fairly dramatic in his opening statement. Although elected prosecuting attorneys usually have an assistant or deputy assist at trial, Russell, for whatever reason, does not.

"Ladies and gentlemen," Russell begins and softens his voice, "come back with me to that Friday the thirteenth in October of last year and visualize the terror that Harriett Porter-Bingham experienced when, sleeping in the eerie gloom at the far end of her mansion in the seldom used guest quarters while the rest of the mansion was being renovated, and being awakened by an intruder rummaging through dresser drawers." Russell pauses. I suspect this gimmick is to give the jury time to absorb the scene.

"Picture if you will, Harriett Bingham bolting upright in bed and alerting the would-be burglar that there was someone else present in the room. Although the only light in the room was a small dresser lamp the intruder had turned on, Mrs. Bingham was able to clearly see a man wearing a Cleveland Indians baseball cap, gloves and dark clothing.

"Can you imagine what raced through her mind knowing she was isolated and that there was no one to cry out to or lend a helping hand—a frail eighty-four year old woman at the mercy of someone who she had never seen before and not sure what he was capable of doing? The evidence will show that terror turned to panic when the intruder flipped on the ceiling light. Obviously noticing Mrs. Bingham for the first time, he immediately stuck a handgun in her face, and with his finger on the trigger, demanded her to lie down and be silent.

"Mrs. Bingham will tell you under oath about the fear she experienced knowing that the only way he could keep her from identifying him was for him to kill her. She will also testify that she was afraid of guns and never had one pointed at her before. She will testify further that she was eyeball-to-eyeball with the intruder and that his face was forever etched in her memory.

"She will testify that the intruder was a man she picked out of both a photographic lineup and a physical or what is sometimes called a police lineup. She will testify that the intruder was Dr. Montel Rudland, the defendant in this case—the man seated here in court next to his attorney, Leland Winthrop." He then points at me. "That man!" Russell says and then sits down.

The courtroom is dead silent for a few moments. Leland leans over and whispers to me, "That opening was unique and most effective."

Judge Grimsley breaks the silence. "Mr. Winthrop, does the defense wish to make an opening statement at this time?"

"No, Your Honor. We will reserve opening until the conclusion of the prosecution's case."

When I look at the jury, I can see Russell's opening had its intended effect. Those members of the jury who had made eye contact before, except for one of the younger women, cease to look at me. Instead they examine their nails or look down at the floor.

"Russell seems to be caught up in his own rhetoric," Leland whispers to me as Russell gets ready to call his first witness.

I nod knowing the honeymoon with Russell is over. "He's obviously pushing for a conviction," I whisper back.

Russell calls as his first witness Detective Kevin Summers. When Summers takes the stand, he appears to be relaxed and confident. He testifies to his and Reynolds' interview with me on October twenty-first, twenty-seventeen. He testifies to me producing a Cleveland Indians baseball cap, a sack containing twenty-three silver dollars with some minted in the 1890s and my Glock 17 handgun. Photographs of those items were introduced into evidence and circulated among the jurors over Leland's objection. Leland had argued that the court's ruling only allowed reference to those items and that the photographs were "tantamount to introducing the items themselves and just as devastating." He further argued, "Even any reference in the witness' testimony to the items should have been precluded because of a lack of a nexus to the crimes themselves. Their probative value is outweighed by their prejudicial effect."

"Why do you suppose the back-tracking?" I write on Leland's legal pad and slide it in front of him.

"Russell's opening!" Leland writes back.

The rest of Summers' testimony is fairly benign (my term). Now, it's Leland's turn to cross-examine.

"Detective Summers, you and fellow detective Lloyd Reynolds you say, investigated the so-called crime scene on Friday, October thirteenth, twenty-seventeen, about eleven o'clock at night, is that correct?"

"Yes."

"Were the two of you doing a double shift that day?"

Summers frowns. "What do you mean"?

"According to the police documents we reviewed, you and Reynolds worked the day shift which was eight to four."

"That's our regular shift."

"But your report of the incident said you and Reynolds responded to a 911 call that same day at around ten p.m."

"Reynolds and I were in charge of the series of burglaries in and around Cleveland and were notified by one of the on-duty detectives of still another burglary and we responded, as was our practice. We reasoned that the intruder at Mrs. Bingham's mansion could very well be the same one who had committed the other burglaries that to this day have remained unsolved."

"Did you think that if you could identify Mrs. Bingham's burglar you could solve the other burglaries?"

Looking smug, Summers replies, "That was a strong possibility."

"Now you and the detective squad at the CPD are known for your proficiency, is that not correct?"

"Yes, it has been said we are a model unit."

"With all the expertise and resources available to your department, did you find anything that tied Dr. Rudland to any of the other burglaries?"

Summers hesitates before answering. "No."

"As a matter of fact, you had no evidence whatsoever that there had even been a break-in or a robbery at the Bingham mansion on the night in question or that a gun had even been pointed in Mrs. Bingham's face—other than her say so, isn't that correct?"

"I suppose you could say so."

"Oh, come now, Detective Summers, you can be more definitive than that. You didn't find any forced entry or point of entry, did you?"

"No."

"You didn't find any strange fingerprints or DNA at the mansion, did you?"

"The would-be burglar wore gloves."

"Just answer the question."

"No," Summers says sharply, "we didn't find any strange fingerprints or DNA."

"Do you know for sure whether there were any coins missing?"

"Only what Mrs. Bingham said was missing."

"Did you see a lot of expensive antiques and decorative items on display at the scene?"

"Yes."

"By the way, Detective Summers, how many silver coins did Mrs. Bingham report missing?"

"Only a few her late husband carried around with him for good luck."

"Maybe four or five?"

"As I recall, she said three." Summers shifts in the witness chair.

"But not twenty-three?"

"No, not likely."

"How many did Dr. Rudland produce when asked?"

"Twenty-three."

"Twenty-three. Did he say where he got them?"

"He said they were given to him by his father."

"How was it he produced them?"

Appearing to think for a moment, Summers finally responds, "I asked him if he had any and when he said yes, I asked him to produce them."

"Were they in a bag along with some other coins?"

"Yes, there were three cards of state quarters."

"Did Mrs. Bingham report any state quarters being taken in the burglary slash robbery?"

"No."

"And the sack holding the silver dollars, did you determine where it came from?"

"From Dr. Rudland's grandmother, as far as we were able to determine."

"Is that the bag that is pictured along with the twenty-three silver dollars marked People's Exhibit 1?"

"Yes."

"Regarding the photographic lineup you testified to on direct, why was Dr. Rudland's picture included?"

"We needed eight photographs and we only had seven so we clipped his picture from an ad for his clinic from the newspaper."

Leland leans forward on one arm resting against the podium. He asks, "Was Dr. Rudland a suspect at the time?"

Summers again shifts in his chair. He appears to be uneasy with the line of questioning. "No, his picture was inserted as a filler."

"Did that photographic lineup contain the photograph of a suspect?"

"Yes."

"Where did the photograph of the suspect and the photographs of the other six come from?"

"From mug shots we took from our files."

"Did some of those seven have facial hair and some not?"

"Yes."

"Didn't Mrs. Bingham also tell you that her assailant had brown eyes and that the two were eyeball-to-eyeball and that she would never forget that face?"

"Yes."

"And what color eyes does Dr. Rudland have?"

"Blue."

"Blue." Leland glances at the jury. "Thank you, Detective Summers. No further questions."

WHEN REYNOLDS TESTIFIED ON direct, it was a long and drawn out ordeal. When Leland cross-examined him, it was sweet and simple.

"Detective Reynolds," Leland begins, "As an advisory witness, you were in court when Detective Summers testified, correct?"

"Yes."

"Was everything he testified to on cross-examination correct?"

"Yes."

"When you and Detective Summers asked Dr. Rudland if he had a Cleveland Indians baseball cap, what did he say."

"He admitted he did."

When Reynolds says 'admitted,' I shudder. How will the jury interpret that?

Leland continues his cross, "And when you asked him if he had one, he didn't deny it, did he?"

"No, he didn't."

"Did you ask him to produce it?"

"No."

"Is that because almost everyone in these parts has a Cleveland Indians baseball cap?"

"Partly."

"He didn't try to hide the fact that he had a coin collection either, did he?"

"No."

"In fact, when you asked him to produce it, he did, didn't he?"

"Yes."

"Detective Reynolds, can you explain how the three silver dollars allegedly taken in the burglary/robbery suddenly became twenty-three?"

"Not really."

"Didn't you think it was important to determine whether Dr. Rudland's collection contained the three silver dollars allegedly taken in the burglary/robbery?"

"Yes."

"Did you ever determine that any of the twenty-three silver dollars were in any way connected to the burglary/robbery?"

"No."

"And even to this day, you have yet to determine that they were in any way connected. Isn't that right, Detective Reynolds?"

"You might say that."

"The same thing was true of the Cleveland Indians baseball cap, correct?"

"Only that the intruder also wore a Cleveland Indians baseball cap."

"Detective Reynolds, tell the jury whether you own a Cleveland Indians baseball cap."

Looking sheepish, Reynold answers in a low tone, "Yes, I have one."

"I didn't hear you."

"Yes, I have a Cleveland Indians baseball cap."

"After you interviewed Dr. Rudland, you didn't place him under arrest, did you?"

"No."

"Isn't that because you weren't sure he was the perpetrator?"

"Yes."

"Even though Mrs. Bingham said he was?"

"Yes, we wanted to be sure."

"Now, did the CPD crime scene investigators ever turn up any fingerprints, DNA, or anything at the scene that could be connected to Dr. Rudland?"

"No."

"Could you speak up, Detective Reynolds?"

"No!"

"When you interviewed Dr. Rudland, did he seem cooperative?"

"Yes."

"Not trying to hide anything?"

"Not as far as I could tell."

"Tell the jury how many of the participants in the police lineup had photographs in the photographic lineup."

"Only one."

"Only one!" Leland glances at the jury. "Who was that?"

Now Reynolds is squirming in the witness chair. He answers in a soft voice, "Dr. Rudland."

"Could you speak louder, please."

"Dr. Rudland!"

"Thank you, Detective. Why did you arrest Dr. Rudland?"

"Mainly because he was identified by an eyewitness."

"Who was that?"

"Mrs. Bingham."

"The same Mrs. Bingham who said the man who pointed the gun in her face had brown eyes and because the two were eyeball-to-eyeball she would never forget his face?"

"Yes."

"By the way, Detective Reynolds, did Mrs. Bingham ever identify any of the twenty-three silver dollars depicted in People's Exhibit 1 as having been taken in the burglary slash robbery?"

"No."

"Not even one?"

"No."

"Did you look at the silver dollars provided by Dr. Rudland?"

"Yes."

"Did any look worn from having been carried around in someone's pockets?"

Reynolds bristles, "I'm no expert, but no it did not appear any were worn."

"Not even one?"

"No."

"Other than your silver service revolver, do you personally have any handguns?"

"If you're asking if I have a Glock 17, the answer is yes."

"What color is it?"

"Black."

"Did you check to see if Dr. Rudland had a criminal record?"

"Of course, we always do."

"And did he?"

"No."

"No criminal record. Thank you, Detective. No further questions."

AFTER THE COURT RECESSES for the day, we head over to Leland's office.

I'm encouraged by the way the cross went and eager to get Leland's slant. "Well?" I say.

"Well, what?" he responds and raises his brows.

"What do you think?"

"What do *you* think?" he asks and peers at me as if I were a hostile witness.

"I…" I can't quite get the words out of my mouth. Stammering is not my trademark, but my anxiety is getting the best of me. Finally, I say, "You did a masterful job of cross and exposed the case for what it is, a farce. I'm just afraid to even believe it's such a lopsided case—and in my favor."

"Thank you, Monty. I've always prided myself in being an effective cross-examiner. I've won cases on cross. Lectured and written about cross. I don't want to appear arrogant or smug but today we made both witnesses look like idiots."

When Leland says that, I'm reminded of Reynolds' remark at the live lineup when Leland protested that I was the only original participant in the group. "That's what a suppression hearing is all about. Tell it to the judge. We're stuck with what we've got…"

Leland jabs the intercom button. "Bring in a bottle of the strongest scotch we have in stock and two glasses with ice." He winks at me, "We just slew the dragon."

THE NEXT DAY, THE prosecution calls Harriett Bingham to the stand. She is assisted by one of the female investigators from Russell's office.

She looks frail as she takes the oath and asks several times for Judge Grimsley to repeat portions before she finally says,

"I do." Despite her social status and wealth, she is a pathetic woman, and I actually feel sorry for her. Facing my accuser for the first time makes me feel powerless and apprehensive. The realization that if the jury believes her, nothing I can do or say will matter. Everything I had worked so hard for my whole life and my whole future now is in the hands of this so-called eyewitness.

Russell does a good job dealing with a hearing impaired witness, and at the same time refraining from asking leading questions which are no-nos on direct examination.

When she is asked if she can identify the man who robbed her on that fateful night, she looks frantically around the courtroom and starts to pick one of the reporters seated in the front row of the spectator section.

"Humph," Judge Grimsley clears his throat, apparently to get Mrs. Bingham's attention. She looks his direction. "Would it help to step down where you can see better?"

"Yes, the lights up here are so bright, they blind me." She picks up her cane and is helped down from the witness stand by the bailiff and is positioned in direct proximity to where I'm seated.

"Yes, that's the man who held the gun on me," she says jabbing in my direction with her cane.

I slump back in my chair. *Surprise, surprise. Déjà vu! Feels like the contrived lineup—all over again.*

Judge Grimsley then asks me to stand. "Is that the man you are pointing to?"

"Yes, that's the man!" And then, as if it were rehearsed, she says, "I'd never forget that face. We were eyeball-to-eyeball. I'd never had a gun poked in my face before!"

"Are you certain he's the man?" Judge Grimsley asks.

"Didn't I just say so?" She asks in a scolding voice—one that is obviously intimidating even to Judge Grimsley.

Leland whispers, "Hell's bells! Any of the rest of us would be immediately hauled off to jail for contempt of court!"

When Leland is given the opportunity to cross-examine Mrs. Bingham, she glares at him. "And who are you, young man," she asks.

"I'm Leland Winthrop. I'm the attorney who is representing Dr. Rudland."

Mrs. Bingham leans forward in her chair, "What kind of doctor is he?"

"He's a medical doctor."

Mrs. Bingham, with a surprised expression, says, "You mean the man who robbed me is a medical doctor? Why, they have more money than God."

Not everyone on the jury laughs—which bothers me.

"Mrs. Bingham, I have just a few questions," Leland says. "In his opening statement, the prosecuting attorney said you were all alone at the time of the robbery."

Mrs. Bingham squints at Leland, "Who said that?"

"Mr. Dawson, the prosecuting attorney who just questioned you." Leland points in Russell's direction.

"I never told him that," Mrs. Bingham bristles. "Why, Nora, my nurse, as I recall was sleeping just across the hall." She squints as if trying to remember.

That comes as a surprise to everyone. When I look across the table at Russell, he's as white as a sheet.

"How is it you never told anybody about that?"

"Nobody asked me. All I was asked by the police was whether there was anyone else in the room at the time I was robbed and I said no."

"How was it Nora didn't come to your aid?"

"You'll have to ask her," Mrs. Bingham says, and smugly tilting her chin up, she gathers her sweater closer around her shoulders and glares at Leland. "Now that I think about it, that was Nora's night off. She did that on occasion, you know."

"How many silver dollars were taken in the robbery?"

"Three. My husband carried those around in his pocket to the day he died. He said they brought him good luck."

"Do you remember when they were minted?"

"Sometime in the 1890s."

"Were they worn?"

"Oh, my yes! They were worn when my husband got them from his father and probably when his father got them from my husband's grandfather."

"Mrs. Bingham, I'm handing you People's exhibit 1 which is a photograph of some silver dollars and a cloth bag."

Mrs. Bingham leans forward and accepts the exhibit.

"Do you recognize any of those coins?"

Mrs. Bingham squints again as she studies the exhibit. She finally looks up at Leland and says, "Can't say that I do. They're all too shinny and new looking. Percy's didn't look anything like any of those. They were one of a kind."

"And the flour bag?"

"Looks pretty ragged, like an old cloth bag."

"Ever seen it before?"

"Not that I know of. Percy's were not in any kind of bag. They were just loose in the top dresser drawer along with some of his items that I stored there."

Leland takes the exhibit from Mrs. Bingham, and as he places it on the exhibit table, he glances at the jury.

"Mrs. Bingham, I see you're wearing glasses. When you came face-to-face with the intruder were you wearing your glasses?"

Mrs. Bingham gives Leland a scathing look and says, "Do people wear glasses when they sleep?"

"Mrs. Bingham, I'm asking whether you were wearing yours at the time of the robbery."

"Of course not! Didn't I just say that?" Mrs. Bingham then glares again at Leland.

"When the police had you view photographs shortly after the incident, did they tell you that they had a suspect?"

"Only that they might have a suspect."

"Thank you, Mrs. Bingham. No further questions of this witness, Your Honor."

Mrs. Bingham is assisted from the witness box, and Leland takes his seat. When he does, he nudges me with his elbow. I nudge back—score one for the good guys.

The prosecution rests its case in chief and now it's our turn.

"Will you be ready after the lunch recess to make your opening statement, Mr. Winthrop?"

"We will, Your Honor," Leland responds.

"Very well, this court will stand adjourned until one-thirty."

AT LUNCH WE ANALYZE Mrs. Bingham's testimony.

"Didn't know judges were supposed to take sides," I say.

"They're not," Leland says and shakes his head. "Not sure what he did rises to the level of improper conduct but it comes damn close. His excuse will be that he was just trying to move the case along and make sure there was no doubt about who was being identified."

"Looked to me like he wanted to make sure the jury didn't think she was unsure."

"I'm sure her focusing in on one of the reporters didn't go unnoticed by the jury. I guess one could argue the distance in court between the two of you was greater than the shorter distance between her and the intruder in the bedroom."

"Why didn't you go into the color of the eyes of the robber?"

"She already told the police, and the detectives testified that she told them they were brown. The jury can see they're blue. Plus you'll be testifying later this afternoon and I'll make sure we get that in."

"LADIES AND GENTLEMEN," LELAND begins his opening statement, "since the prosecution has the burden of proving Dr. Rudland's guilt, they go first. You've already heard what the prosecution said they would prove; now it's our turn even though we don't have to prove anything.

"Although Dr. Rudland has a constitutional right not to testify, he will. In fact, he will be the only witness to testify for the defense. He will testify that on Friday, October thirteenth, two thousand and seventeen, he returned home after an eventful day at the medical clinic where he was employed. He will testify that he showered and warmed a dinner his wife prepared prior to her leaving with their three children to spend the weekend with her sister and family in Akron.

"Dr. Rudland will testify he didn't make the trip because he was on call that weekend at the clinic. He will further testify that from the time he arrived home until six-thirty a.m. the following day, he remained home. He will testify that he spent the evening reading a novel and that he retired sometime around ten or ten-thirty. He will testify that he had never met Mrs. Bingham, and even though he and his family bicycled past her mansion occasionally, he had never been inside. He will testify that he had a thriving medical practice; was financially secure; was a Cleveland Indians baseball fan and that he and his two

JUDITH BLEVINS & CARROLL MULTZ

sons each had a Cleveland Indians baseball cap; that he had twenty-three uncirculated silver dollars minted in the 1890s that his father had given him and a Glock 17 pistol he seldom used that was kept in his desk drawer.

"After you have heard Dr. Rudland's testimony, you will conclude that Dr. Rudland did not rob Mrs. Bingham, didn't burglarize her residence or stick a gun in her face. Since Dr. Rudland had no motive and the prosecution has not proven otherwise, we will be asking you at the conclusion of the case to return not guilty verdicts on each of the three counts."

When Leland announces that I'm to be called as a witness, Judge Grimsley grills me on whether I want to waive my constitutional right to remain silent.

"Do you realize you don't have to testify and can't be forced to do so?"

"Yes."

"That the Fifth Amendment to the United States Constitution offers you that right?"

"Yes."

"That you are presumed to be innocent and that that presumption prevails unless and until the prosecution proves by sufficient evidence that you are guilty beyond a reasonable doubt?"

"Yes."

"Knowing all of that, is it still your desire to testify?"

"Yes."

"Is anyone forcing you to testify?"

"No."

"Is your willingness to testify a free and voluntary act on your part?"

"Yes."

"The court finds that Dr. Rudland has made a knowing, intelligent and voluntary waiver of his constitutional rights."

I'm then sworn in and directed by Judge Grimsley to be seated at the witness stand.

After Leland asks me my name, address and occupation, he asks me where I attended college, medical school and where I did my residency.

"If my math is correct," he says, "you spent eleven years after high school to be equipped to be a medical doctor?"

"Yes."

"Where are you licensed to practice medicine?"

"In the states of Ohio and Iowa."

"Are you affiliated with any medical center?"

"Yes, Talman Medical Center here in Cleveland."

"How long have you been employed there?"

"Going on fourteen years."

"What is your yearly income?"

"Roughly two hundred and twenty-five thousand dollars."

"Roughly a quarter million?"

"Yes."

"Guess I should have gone to medical school"

Even Judge Grimsley chuckles.

"Do you owe anything on student loans or have a mortgage on your home?"

"No. My parents helped me with what scholarships didn't cover and my wife's parents as well as mine helped us purchase our home."

"Are you financially secure?"

"Yes, we're fortunate not to be in debt."

"How old are you?"

"Turned forty-four in August."

"Do you know Harriett Porter-Bingham?"

"No, not personally."

"Are you familiar with her residence?"

"Rode past her home with my wife and kids on occasion. We live not quite three miles from her mansion in Shaker Heights."

"Ever been on the premises?"

"Never."

"Were you anywhere near the premises on Friday, October thirteenth, two thousand and seventeen?"

"No."

"Did you rob Mrs. Bingham at gunpoint?"

"Absolutely not."

"Tell the jury what you did from the time you arrived home from the clinic on Friday, October thirteenth, two thousand and seventeen, until you awoke the following morning."

I then relate what I did as outlined in Leland's opening statement as well as why I didn't make the trip to Akron with my family that weekend.

"Do you own a Cleveland Indians baseball cap?"

"I'm a Cleveland Indians baseball fan as are my two sons. All three of us have a Cleveland Indians baseball cap."

"What color are your eyes?"

"Blue."

"Ever worn contacts?"

"No."

"Where'd you get the silver dollars you turned over to the police?"

"From my father."

"Were you truthful when you told Detectives Summers and Reynolds you didn't do what you've been accused of doing?"

"Yes."

"Have you told the truth today under oath?"

"Yes."

"No further questions," Leland says.

When it is Russell's turn to cross-examine, he announces he has only one question.

"Dr. Rudland, other than your contention that you didn't commit the crimes for which you've been charged, do you have any evidence to show you didn't?"

Leland is immediately on his feet. "Objection! Your Honor, in an American courtroom an accused doesn't have to prove anything. It's up to the prosecution to prove an accused's guilt, not up to an accused to prove his innocence. Besides, how do you prove a negative?"

"Objection overruled," Judge Grimsley says. "This is cross-examination and a proper avenue for Mr. Dawson to explore."

"Would you like for me to repeat the question?" Russell asks.

I'm so stunned at the judge's ruling, I can't think straight. "Yes, please," I reply.

"Dr. Rudland, other than your contention that you didn't commit the crimes for which you've been charged, do you have any evidence to prove you didn't?"

"No more than Mrs. Bingham has to show I did."

Russell blanches. "No further questions," he says.

I was afraid I'd committed a *faux paus* and I glance at Leland. He's smiling broadly.

"Dr. Rudland, you may step down," Judge Grimsley says. Turning to Leland, he asks, "Mr. Winthrop, will you be calling any other witnesses?"

"Your Honor, may I have a minute?"

Back at the defense table, I huddle with Leland. "We have Carissa endorsed as a witness," he whispers, "we hadn't intended to call her. All she can do is confirm that she and your kids were gone that weekend and you were home alone. From the prosecution's standpoint, that reinforces opportunity."

"I don't want to involve her in this, even if her testimony would be helpful," I whisper back. "Regardless, we don't want to emphasize my lack of an alibi as you and I have already decided."

"Your Honor, we have no other witnesses to call," Leland says. "The defense rests its case."

"Thank you, Mr. Winthrop," Judge Grimsley says and turning to Russell, asks, "Any rebuttal, Mr. Dawson?"

"No, Your Honor," Russell responds.

"Very well," Judge Grimsley says, and removing his glasses, addresses the jury. "Ladies and gentlemen, both sides have rested. That means all the evidence has been presented. The attorneys and I will be using the remainder of the day to prepare the final instructions on the law. Those will be given to you tomorrow, followed by final arguments and then your deliberation and return of a verdict.

"You will be released for the day to return here tomorrow promptly at eight a.m. In the interim, I give you the usual admonition not to discuss this case among yourselves or with anyone else and not to expose yourself to any press coverage about the case."

To the attorneys, Judge Grimsley says, "Meet me in chambers."

After Judge Grimsley leaves the courtroom, Leland tells me that he will call me later in the day. Previously, he had advised me that only attorneys meet with the judge to prepare instructions.

Leland called late afternoon to inform me that all went well with the instructions as most had been prepared in advance by the attorneys and that he would meet me tomorrow at the courthouse at seven-thirty a.m.

"HEY, SLUGGER," CARISSA SAYS, as I wipe sleep from my eyes. "You're getting to be quite the celebrity."

I amble out of bed, and like the Pied Piper, Carissa leads me to the kitchen where a steaming cup of coffee and the morning edition of the *Cleveland Daily Bugle* await me.

ACCUSER CONFRONTS ACCUSED IN OPEN COURT

Courtroom drama unfolded Wednesday when heiress Harriett Porter-Bingham pointed out her assailant to the jury in the prosecution of physician and former football star, Dr. Montel Rudland. "That's the man. I'll never forget that face. We were eyeball-to-eyeball. I never had a gun poked in my face before." When asked by Judge Ian Grimsley if she was sure, the spunky eyewitness said, "Yes, that's the man who held the gun on me."

The prosecution rested their case after calling only three witnesses, CPD Detectives Kevin Summers and Lloyd Reynolds and Mrs. Bingham. The previous day, Summers and Reynolds testified that Dr. Rudland had been identified by Mrs. Bingham from a photographic lineup where his photograph had been clipped from an advertisement for his medical clinic and inserted as a filler.

When asked by Dr. Rudland's attorney, Leland Winthrop, if his client was a suspect at the time both detectives answered no.

According to the detectives' testimony, Mrs. Bingham picked Dr. Rudland out of a police lineup. On cross-examination both detectives admitted that Dr. Rudland was the only one to appear photographically and in person in both lineups. Winthrop had tried unsuccessfully to have the out-

of-court and the in-court identifications suppressed on the grounds that the first lineup was unduly suggestive and the subsequent lineups were tainted by the previous lineups.

Late yesterday, Dr. Rudland was called as the sole witness for the defense. He claimed to be home at the time of the alleged burglary and robbery and denied any involvement. When asked by prosecutor Russell Dawson if anyone could vouch for his whereabouts at the time of the break-in, he stated his wife and their three children were out of town at the time. When asked by Dawson if he had evidence to substantiate his contention that he didn't do it, he said, "No more than Mrs. Bingham has to show that I did."

The jury was excused to later this morning when the jury will be instructed on the law and both sides will make final arguments. It is expected jury deliberations will commence late in the forenoon.

"Not the kind of press I'm used to or particularly relish," I say, as I polish off a Danish. I shave and take a quick shower and hop in the clothes Carissa has laid out for me.

"I'll be praying for you," Carissa says as I give her a peck on the cheek. "Call me when the case goes to the jury."

THE COURTROOM IS STARTING to fill up when I arrive. Leland is already there with a copy of the instructions and an outline of his final argument. "Here, read this," he says as he shoves the instructions toward me.

When I see how many there are, I say, "How can jurors remember all of this?"

"They'll each get a copy to take into the jury room."

Reading through the instructions, I'm surprised they're easy to understand. When I'm halfway through, Leland says,

"They're written in layman language. Now even lawyers can understand them."

The jurors are seated and the courtroom is called to order as Judge Grimsley enters. We all stand. "Please be seated," he directs. Wasting no time, he adjusts his glasses and reads the stack of instructions out loud. When finished, he asks Russell if he is ready to give his final argument.

My whole life is on the line and I'm a complete wreck as I watch with trepidation. Russell nods, stands, and buttoning his suit jacket, he strolls to the podium.

"Ladies and gentlemen of the jury, before giving my final argument I'd like to take this opportunity to thank each of you for serving as jurors in this case. The role jurors play in our system of justice is just as important as that of the judges and attorneys. Soon the role you will play in deciding whether to convict or not convict will be the most important of all.

"This case boils down to he said—she said. If you believe Harriett Porter-Bingham, you should convict. If you believe Dr. Montel Rudland, you should acquit.

"What evidence do we have that points to guilt other than the eyewitness account of Mrs. Bingham? That's a fair question you should be asking and one that I would ask if I were on the jury. Does the physical description given of the perpetrator of the crimes charged match the physical description of Dr. Rudland? Pretty close wouldn't you say, when you consider Mrs. Bingham was not standing when she estimated the height and weight of the perpetrator? And the lighting in the room could very well have made Dr. Rudland's blue eyes appear dark or brown in color.

"If you were awakened from a sound sleep and found a burglar in your room rummaging in dresser drawers, that image would forever be etched in your mind as it was in Mrs.

Bingham's mind. And if you never had a gun stuck in your face and were eyeball-to-eyeball with an unmasked intruder with his finger on the trigger, not knowing if that was the last image you'd ever see, that image would forever be etched in your mind as well. A face you'd never forget. A face you'd remember if you saw it again.

"The baseball cap is significant not because everyone in Cleveland has a Cleveland Indians baseball cap but because the perpetrator was wearing one and Dr. Rudland, who lived only a few miles from Mrs. Bingham, had one. The silver dollars minted in the 1890s taken in the burglary slash robbery are not significant in and of themselves but the fact that Dr. Rudland also had silver dollars is. And the fact that the Glock 17 pistol taken from Dr. Rudland's residence matched that described by Mrs. Bingham also has significance. Maybe singly none of those items spell guilt, collectively with an eyewitness account they do spell guilt.

"Did it appear to be a coincidence that Dr. Rudland's wife and family just happened to be out of town when the crimes were committed or that Mrs. Bingham's residence was only a few miles away from Dr. Rudland's residence—a distance that could easily be covered by a bicycle in a matter of a few minutes?

"Why didn't the intruder wear a mask or some disguise you might ask? With the Bingham mansion being renovated, an intruder could easily conclude it was not occupied. From the evidence, it was evident that Mrs. Bingham was not the only one who was startled.

"When you review the evidence in its totality and the improbability of all the coincidences, you will have no difficulty in returning a guilty verdict to all three counts. And that's what we're asking that you do."

Russell pauses a few moments before gathering his notes and returning to the prosecution's table. The courtroom is so hushed you could hear a pin drop. I'm devastated! After that final argument, I'm ready to convict myself. I look at Leland. He probably sees the terror in my eyes and pats my arm. "Have faith," he whispers. "We've just begun to fight."

"Mr. Winthrop, you may make your final argument now." Judge Grimsley removes his glasses and massages one eye with the heel of his hand.

Leland looks relaxed as he moves to the podium. He has no notes or documents of any kind. He begins, "Ladies and gentlemen of the jury, the defense would also thank each of you for sitting in judgment in this case. Notice there's not a lot of evidence to sift through. In fact, that is the problem from the prosecutor's standpoint. And I can tell you that with some authority having been a prosecutor myself.

"Mr. Dawson hangs his whole case on the so-called eyewitness, an eyewitness whose recollection is flawed. He talks about coincidences. He missed recounting perhaps the most glaring coincidence of all—an identification of a so-called perpetrator of a crime whose photograph was clipped from a newspaper ad placed by a clinic containing the photographs of the physicians employed at the clinic. The police could have picked from an assortment of ads for everything from dental clinics to law firms to insurance agencies to real estate companies. No, they picked one from Talman Medical Center. Of the more than a dozen specialists pictured in the ad, they picked the photograph of Dr. Montel Rudland, the defendant in this case. According to the testimony of Detectives Summers and Reynolds, they needed another photograph as a filler so that they had a composite of eight mug shots. The other seven were taken from a data base the police had on file."

Turning to me, Leland says, "Dr. Rudland would you please stand and face the jury." When I do, he says to the jury, "Do you see anything remarkable about Dr. Rudland's face? Does he remind you of anyone? Perhaps a teacher you had or a former classmate or maybe a neighbor or even a relative? Are there any distinguishing scars, tattoos, piercings, missing teeth, distorted features of any kind that would set him apart from the thousands of people you pass on the streets of Cleveland every day?"

"You may be seated," he says to me. "The only thing that might not be a coincidence is Mrs. Bingham's selecting Dr. Rudland from the police lineup. After all, he's the only one to have appeared in both out-of-court lineups and who had already been identified by Mrs. Bingham. And how about his identification in open court by Mrs. Bingham who almost identified one of the reporters who was seated in the front row of the spectator section as being the perpetrator? Remember, this was by a so-called eyewitness who said she'd never forget the face of the man who pointed a gun in her face. It wasn't until she was escorted from the witness stand and placed in front of Dr. Rudland that she said he was the man. Since neither Mr. Dawson nor I look anything like Dr. Rudland, who was she going to pick? It is up to you, ladies and gentlemen, to decide whether the out-of court identifications and the in-court identification were unduly suggestive. And if you looked closely at Dr. Rudland's eyes, you no doubt observed they were blue—blue as the sky on a clear day—and not brown as Mrs. Bingham had described them to the police shortly after the incident.

"Mr. Dawson makes it appear that it is an oddity that anyone would have a Cleveland Indians baseball cap, a coin collection containing 1890 silver dollars and a handgun the color of the one Mrs. Bingham said was brandished by the perpetrator.

I don't know if you noticed, but several jurors in the jury pool wore Cleveland Indian baseball caps to court the first day. And isn't it a miracle that three silver dollars taken in the robbery grew to twenty-three. Sounds like the biblical account of the loaves and fishes.

"Speaking of defying the odds and the Bible, who would risk his freedom, reputation, career and family for a few pieces of silver? What fool would risk a lot for a little? It was four years of college, four years of medical school and three years of residency that was supposedly traded.

"When I was a prosecuting attorney just starting my legal career, I was taught that a prosecuting attorney had to prove means, motive and opportunity. I guess you could argue Dr. Rudland had the opportunity in this case and maybe even the means to commit the crimes. However, the prosecution didn't prove motive. Dr. Rudland was financially secure; he didn't need the money. He had an annual income of about a quarter-million dollars and financial backing from both sides of the family. What then? Greed or maybe a thrill? In rebuttal, Mr. Dawson may argue that, but that calls for speculation and conjecture and is not supportable by the evidence. In layman terms, it is called an absurd argument.

"Since the prosecution has the burden of proof in this case, they go first and last. This is my last and only opportunity to address you. They have what is called rebuttal argument still remaining. In assessing the evidence, remember the evidence presented by the prosecution cannot be based on speculation and conjecture but on credible evidence that convinces you of Dr. Rudland's guilt beyond a reasonable doubt.

"The likelihood that Dr. Rudland, a respected physician and member of our community and a man with absolutely no criminal record and whose photograph was inserted in a lineup with a den of misfits as the perpetrator is one in a trillion—trillion. The likelihood of mistaken identification, therefore, is great considering the circumstances. Therefore, I'm asking you to return not guilty verdicts on all three counts, not because I'm asking that you do so but because justice requires it."

Leland joins me at the defense's table and once again the courtroom is silent. I have to restrain myself from giving him a high-five. *Maybe I have a chance after all.*

"Mr. Dawson, any rebuttal?"

In his rebuttal argument, Russell addresses the issue of motive. "Self-indulgence breeds piggishness and intemperance," Russell begins. "Dr. Rudland had it all, a thriving medical practice, an expensive home in Shaker Heights, notoriety as a former football star, a family I assume he was proud of and no doubt a beautiful wife. Apparently, he needed more. Fame and fortune were not enough. Greed is not just reserved to lords and kings but to those who have tasted power and affluence. It is difficult to determine why a person would jeopardize it all by one roll of the dice. Sometimes you win and sometimes you lose. It's not up to the prosecution to prove *why* Dr. Rudland did what he did, only to prove that he did it."

CHAPTER 10
THE VERDICT

After the jury has been sent out to deliberate, I'm numb. I'm afraid to get my hopes up. After my experience with the grand jury, I hope for the best but prepare for the worst.

When Judge Grimsley's clerk asks where we can be reached in the event of a verdict, Leland gives her his phone number. "Dr. Rudland will be with me," he says.

"It's doubtful they'll have a verdict anytime soon," Leland says to me as he checks his cellphone. "It's almost four now and they'll barely have time to select a foreman, let alone time to deliberate. If they haven't reached a verdict by six, Judge Grimsley will send them home with instructions to return back here tomorrow to resume deliberations. On the off-chance they reach a decision or are on the verge of reaching a decision, I suggest we meet at my office and we can wait together. We can even send out for dinner if you wish."

When I hesitate, Leland says, "Don't worry, you'll not be charged for the downtime."

"I'll give Carissa a call on my cell and meet you back at your office. What do I tell her when she asks how things went?"

"Tell her I said it's impossible to guess what a jury will do with much accuracy but that I said the odds were seventy-five to twenty-five in your favor and maybe better. With a better jury and an unbiased judge, neither of which we had much control over, I would say it's not too early to uncork the champagne."

I wish some of that confidence would rub off on me.

When I arrive at Leland's office, I can tell he is not at all anxious to sort through the mail that has stacked up on his desk. "I can't focus on anything but the outcome of your case," he says. "I fought for justice as a prosecutor and I fight for justice as a defense attorney. When I left the prosecutor's office I was asked by my students who were majoring in police science how I could switch sides. My pat answer then and now is that I've never switched sides, I'm still on the side of justice."

When Leland doesn't even crack a smile, I know he means it. I'm still trying to second-guess the decision to prosecute, so I ask, "Would you have prosecuted a case like mine?"

"Unlikely, or would probably have presented it to a grand jury like Russell did and left the decision up to your peers rather than play God."

"Would the fact that I passed the polygraph have much bearing?"

"The real question is whether I'd have Mrs. Bingham take a polygraph. I think she would pass it as well. She's convinced you were the perpetrator and that's due in part to a flawed procedure some departments follow in using lineups. Some use an expanded version by having the victim sort through a myriad of photographs in their data system and others try to match the description given by the victim to participants who closely resemble that description. I think the police zeroed in on a suspect and in their haste to solve the crime threw your photograph in just to expedite the process. I think it's a case of meant well, just made a bad choice and you got caught in the middle."

Leland's matter of fact statement to the effect that someone made a bad choice and I got caught in the middle does little to ease the life altering dilemma I'm now facing. "I thought eyewitness testimony was the most reliable."

"Not anymore. When I first started prosecuting cases, during jury selection, we made it a point to make sure jurors realized that circumstantial evidence, such as fingerprints and DNA, were *just as good* as eyewitness testimony. With the advancement of DNA analysis, which has resulted in a number of convictions based on eyewitness testimony being overturned, it appears circumstantial evidence is the *more* reliable of the two. Unfortunately, there's no circumstantial evidence in your case to either refute or corroborate the eyewitness testimony."

"Neither of us can prove who is right." I say. "Neither of us can corroborate our claims—she that I did it and me that I didn't. Doesn't the tie go to the defendant?"

"Theoretically, that's true. However, seldom do defendants get on the stand and say they did it. There are already two strikes against you just by the mere accusation. Remember what Mr. McCabe said during jury selection, 'Where there's smoke, there's fire?' You wouldn't have been charged if you hadn't done something. The mere denial is not enough with some jurors. As I said, they expect defendants to lie to save their skin. When it's an accused's word against the word of the accuser, especially someone like Mrs. Bingham, a jury is more apt to believe the accuser."

I'm doomed! What happened to Leland's prediction, 'I would say it's not too early to uncork the champagne?' "Sounds like I've been lumped in the category of a criminal and once so branded have no avenue of escape. Even if I'm fortunate enough to be acquitted, won't there always be that lingering doubt that I did it and bought my way out?"

"I guess that's the way Mrs. Hildebrand sizes up the criminal justice system."

"If either Mrs. Hildebrand or Mr. McCabe is elected foreperson, he or she won't even have to announce the verdict in order for us to know what it will be."

Before Leland can respond, Brenda is on the intercom. "Sorry to interrupt, Mr. Winthrop. Judge Grimsley's clerk just called saying the jury has been sent home without having reached a verdict. They have been ordered to return at eight a.m. tomorrow to resume deliberations."

Dammit! Another sleepless night!

"HOW'D IT GO, SLUGGER?" Carissa asks when I arrive home.

"Take it you didn't watch any of the local news channels."

"You know I've deliberately avoided watching the local news this past week. Don't want to be upset with the slanted views. I have to distance myself to keep my sanity."

"Russell acts as though he wants my head on a platter. In his rebuttal argument he painted me as someone obsessed with power and money. He said my motive was greed—always wanting more."

Carissa tucks her legs up under her and pats the spot next to her on the sofa beckoning me to sit. "Kind of like the pot calling the kettle black, don't you think? You pale in comparison to his so-called victim in that department, I would say."

"Russell has the ability to twist everything we say."

"That's what lawyers get paid to do."

"He had a retort for everything and painted me as a villain. Guess the results from my polygraph didn't mean much."

"A hapless little old lady pitted against a brute is going to win the sympathy of the jury every time. The cards were stacked against you from the start."

I sink further into the cushions. Both Carissa and Leland are making me feel like I should pack my duffel and head for parts unknown before it's too late. "Isn't it amazing that I'm painted as a poor little rich boy with an insatiable appetite and she, worth millions, is to be pitied?"

"Wonder what Russell would have said if you had been a day laborer having ten kids and a difficult time making ends meet."

"You know what his argument would have been. See, no matter what we argued, Russell would have twisted it to show motive."

WHEN I WAKE UP that balmy Friday morning I look at the digital clock on the night stand. It is almost eight-thirty a.m. I jump up with a start forgetting for the moment that I don't have to be in court at eight. Between a night filled with bad dreams and anxiety over the outcome of my case, I'm a little disoriented. I sit on the edge of my bed trying to get my bearings. When I smell the aroma of coffee and homemade cinnamon rolls, I move in the direction of the kitchen. I'm met in the hall by Carissa.

"Hey sleepyhead, thought you were gonna sleep all day."

I'm still wiping sleep from my eyes as she puts her arms around my neck. "I've become used to having you around in the mornings—except for this week, that is."

"I guess being on administrative leave does have its perks. As for this week, it's all been a blur. Tell me all of this is just a bad dream."

"It's called life," Carissa says and releases her hold on me momentarily. When I stand frozen in space, she grabs my hand urging me forward and says, "Come on, Slugger. Fresh brewed coffee and cinnamon rolls hot out of the oven await you."

She doesn't have to ask me twice. I let her lead me and when we reach the kitchen, seeing the folded paper next to my place, I say, "Did we make the front page again?"

"It's not a bad article for a change. It's more fair and balanced."

The article in the March ninth edition of the *Cleveland Daily Bugle* reads:

JURY COMMENCES DELIBERATION IN ROBBERY OF HEIRESS

The armed robbery case involving heiress Harriett Porter-Bingham ensued in earnest on Thursday with the attorneys on both sides making their final arguments. In the fourth day of trial, the accused, Dr. Montel Rudland, a local physician and former football star, sat expressionless as prosecuting attorney, Russell Dawson recounted the evidence.

Dawson, anticipating defense's final argument, addressed both the strengths and weaknesses in the prosecution's case. In addressing the defense's claim of misidentification, Dawson argued, "If you were awakened from a sound sleep and found a burglar in your room rummaging through dresser drawers, that image would forever be etched in your mind as it was in Mrs. Bingham's mind. And if you never had a gun stuck in your face and were eyeball-to-eyeball with an unmasked intruder with his finger on the trigger, not knowing if that was the last image you'd ever see, that image would forever be etched in your mind as well."

Dr. Rudland's attorney, Leland Winthrop, in attacking his client's in-court identification by Mrs. Bingham, argued that it was flawed and reminded the jury that she almost identified one of the reporters who was seated in the courtroom as being the perpetrator. "Remember," Winthrop argued, "this was by a so-called eyewitness who said she'd never forget the face of the man who pointed a gun inher face. It wasn't until she was escorted from the witness stand and placed in front of Dr. Rudland, that she said he was the man."

After two hours of deliberation, without reaching a decision, the jury was excused for the day by presiding Judge Ian Grimsley and instructed to return at 8:00 a.m. this morning to resume deliberations.

"Well?" Carissa says.

"Well what?" I reply as I fold the paper and set it aside.

"Does it sound anything like what happened in court yesterday?"

I nod. "I wish we could have let the jury know I passed the polygraph."

"Seems like a waste of money since the results can't be used either for or against an accused."

"Right! And even when an accused passes, it appears that the cops just ignore the results if they don't coincide with their assessment of the case. Guess my passing got my hopes up and agonizing over the fact that we can't use it in my defense is just a waste of time. Hell, I'm not grasping at straws. In my case, there are no straws to grasp. It's pretty much cut and dried."

Carissa caresses my hand across the table. "Don't you dare quit on me! It's not over yet and even if you're found guilty, you will most likely win on appeal."

"Sure. And how much more of our lives are we going to have to sacrifice waiting for the appeal to be heard by the Supreme Court—which I understand moves at a snail's pace?"

"Stop it right now! I'm not going to contribute to your wallowing in self-pity. You're not the only one affected by this trip to hell. Mine and the kids' lives have also been turned wrong side out…"

We both break down and weep. After a few moments, Carissa dabs at her eyes and asks, "How long do you think the jury will be out?"

"No telling," I manage to say. "Leland thought it wouldn't be until late afternoon at the earliest."

"What happens if they still haven't reached a verdict?"

"They'll probably be required to come back tomorrow, at least according to Leland."

I notice a quizzical look cross Carissa's face as she says, "But tomorrow's Saturday."

"Leland said that wouldn't make a difference."

"How about Sunday?"

"Don't know. They would probably have to come back on Monday."

"Okay. So what's the plan?"

"Leland said if we hadn't heard anything by lunch time for me to come by his office and wait for a call from the court."

"I'd like to be there. Want me to go with you?"

"Nah. I'll give you a call when I hear anything."

"Okay, you'd better. You're not the only one on pins and needles…"

"No, but I'm the only one going to prison," I say, and regret saying it as soon as the words leave my mouth.

AFTER LUNCH, I HEAD for Leland's office and run into him just as he returns from lunch. "Heard anything?" I ask and watch him pickup his messages and a stack of files from Brenda's desk."

"Nary a thing." he responds. "Come wait in my office with me. You can either read or watch me work. I'm guessing we won't have a verdict until sometime late afternoon."

I pick up several magazines from the rack in the waiting room and follow Leland into his office. "Tell Brenda what you'd like to drink when she comes in with the mail."

Brenda comes and goes and a couple of hours pass. About midafternoon Leland starts pacing.

"You nervous, too?" I ask.

"This is the worse part of trial work," Leland responds, "waiting for the verdict."

I toss the magazine I'd been thumbing through aside, "Any inkling as to what the verdict will be?"

"Ha! If I knew what a jury would do, I'd go buy some lottery tickets. I'm never sure and the longer they're out usually the more I worry. Although a hung jury would be better than a guilty verdict. The ones you think you win you lose and the ones you think you lose you win."

I'm sorry I asked. Leland's statements did little to lower my anxiety—which is now off the charts. "What happens if they can't reach a unanimous verdict?"

"Judge Grimsley declares a mistrial and we start all over again. By the way, I have Brenda holding all my calls except ones from the court." Leland glances at the phone as if willing it to ring. "We'll know one way or another by five whether they've reached a verdict. If they haven't reached a verdict by then, Judge Grimsley usually has the bailiff interrupt their deliberations to see if they're close to reaching a decision. If they are, he'll go as late as seven to wait for a verdict. If they're not close, he'll have them come back tomorrow and continue their deliberations."

We both jump when the phone rings at four forty-five. Leland grabs up the receiver and I watch his face sag. As soon as he hangs up, he says, "That was Judge Grimsley's clerk. She said the jury was deadlocked and not close to reaching a verdict and had been released to resume deliberations again tomorrow morning."

I immediately call Carissa and advise her of the latest. I can hear disappointment in her voice. However she covers nicely as she says, "I fixed your favorite meal and have some bubbly on ice. Call it an early victory celebration."

"How did you know I was craving prime rib?"

"A woman's intuition, and besides you're pretty predictable. Dinner will be ready when you get home."

When I say goodbye to Leland, he tells me to stay by the phone.

"I'm used to being on call," I say, and head for home and there seek refuge. This may very well be my last night of freedom.

The Saturday edition of the *Cleveland Daily Bugle*, enamored with my trial, again makes it breaking news. The headlines and featured story read as follows:

JURY DEADLOCKED IN ARMED ROBBERY CASE

The jury was excused today to resume deliberations in the prosecution of Dr. Montel Rudland who was charged in the burglary and robbery of heiress Harriett Porter-Bingham. At the end of the day on Thursday and again Friday, the jury announced they were unable to reach a verdict.

During cross-examination of Mrs. Bingham by defense attorney, Leland Winthrop, on Wednesday, her in-court identification of Dr. Rudland was made suspect because of a claim that it was tainted by two "unduly suggestive" out-of-court lineups. Winthrop, in his final argument to the jury on Thursday, argued that Mrs. Bingham had identified the robber as having brown eyes when, in fact, the defendant's eyes were blue. When asked to point out the person who robbed her, she zeroed in on a reporter sitting in the spectator section of the courtroom before identifying the defendant.

When the jury was excused on Friday, Judge Grimsley gave the jury a modified version of the Allen charge or what is sometimes referred to as the dynamite charge or shotgun instruction. It says in part: "If you fail to agree upon a verdict, the case will be left open and may have to be tried again… There is no reason to believe that the case can be tried again by either side any better or more exhaustively than it has been tried before you… There is no reason to believe that the case could ever be submitted to twelve men and women more conscientious, more impartial, or more competent than you… If a substantial majority of your number are in favor of a conviction or an acquittal, those of you who disagree should reconsider… Remember at all times that no juror is expected to give up an honest belief he or she may have but after full deliberation and consideration of the evidence in the case, it is your duty to agree upon a verdict if you can do so."

CARISSA DRIVES ME TO Leland's office at his suggestion. "In the event you are found guilty the court may revoke your bond and you'll end up in the slammer. If you are found not guilty or your PR bond is continued until sentencing, I'll drive you home."

It is midafternoon before the call comes in that the jury has reached a verdict. My heart beats faster than a jungle drum. I'm more nervous than I was when I asked Carrisa to marry me. The day of reckoning has arrived.

"Think positive!" Leland says as he drives me to the courthouse. "The vultures have arrived," he says as we park and make our way through the swarm of reporters and camera crews. About every other step, we are met by a reporter who sticks a microphone in our face. "Any predictions?"

"Any idea how the jury will rule?"

"Will you sue if it's a not guilty verdict?"

"Will you appeal if it's a guilty verdict?"

"What do you think your chances would be?"

"If you're found not guilty will you stay in the community?"

The questions never end and the closer we get to the courtroom, the more nervous I become. Please God, don't abandon me now, I pray.

WHILE WE WAIT FOR the judge and the jury, Russell comes over and extends his hand to Leland. Leland stands and they exchange compliments on the other's courtroom performance. I detect a quiver in Russell's voice as he and Leland speak. I think he's more interested in a win than seeking justice. To him it's a contest; to me it's my whole life. He'll have other cases to try. Me, everything rides on this one case. And this one case rides solely on the testimony of an eyewitness who, if she is mistaken, will never know the difference. The suspense is almost too much to bear.

When the jury is brought in, my heart skips a beat when I see Mr. McCabe carrying what I surmise are the verdict forms. *I knew it!*

"Not a good omen!" Leland whispers. I shake my head.

The bailiff instructs all to stand as Judge Grimsley enters the courtroom. "You all may be seated," the bailiff says. After Judge Grimsley positions himself and arranges his bevy of files on the glass-top desk, he looks at the prosecution table and then at Leland and me at the defense table and says, "Let the record reflect that Mr. Dawson is present in court representing the prosecution and that Dr. Rudland, the defendant, is present along with his attorney, Mr. Winthrop."

When he sees several reporters taking photographs with their cellphones, he's most irritated. "Save the picture-taking for outside the courtroom if you don't want to be removed."

"Are both sides ready to proceed?" he asks Russell and Leland. Both announce they are.

"I understand the jury has reached a verdict," he says.

Mr. McCabe stands with the verdict forms in hand and announces, "We have, Your Honor."

"Very well! Please hand them to the bailiff if you will." Mr. McCabe obliges. The bailiff then carries them to the bench and hands them to the judge. Judge Grimsley examines them and beckons the clerk and when she comes forth he hands them to her. "The clerk will now read the verdicts," he says and orders me to stand.

When I'm found guilty on all three counts, my mind takes me in the direction of Carissa, Jayden, Jennifer and Paxton, then my parents and Carissa's parents. Whether I'm going to prison and lose my medical license only enters my mind later.

"Mr. Winthrop, would you like the jury to be polled?" Judge Grimsley asks.

"We would, Your Honor."

Judge Grimsley then asks each juror, "Was and is this your verdict?" Each answers, "Yes." The jury is then excused with the usual admonition which includes the thanks of the court and permission to discuss the case with whomever they wish.

After the jury is excused, Leland is asked if the defense wants to make the usual motion for judgment of acquittal notwithstanding the verdict.

"We do, Your Honor. We also ask that you reconsider our motion to dismiss the felony assault charge on the grounds that it is the lesser included charge of aggravated robbery which requires the use of a weapon during its commission. At the suppression hearing, we argued submission to the jury of multiple charges arising out of the same conduct was tantamount to Dr. Rudland being charged twice for the same offense—a violation of the double jeopardy clause of the Fifth Amendment to the United States Constitution. You denied our motion, ruling that the defense would have to wait to see if the jury came back with guilty verdicts on both counts. That having happened, we're asking you to set aside the guilty verdict on the felony assault charge and dismiss that charge."

"Any objection, Mr. Dawson?"

"No, Your Honor."

"The court will vacate the guilty verdict on the felony assault charge and issue an order of dismissal. The court will formally enter judgment of conviction on the other two charges. Anything further, Mr. Winthrop?"

"Yes, Your Honor, we ask that Dr. Rudland's bond be continued to sentencing."

"Any objection, Mr. Dawson?"

"No, Your Honor."

"Very well, sentencing will be continued to Friday, March sixteenth, twenty-eighteen, at ten a.m. to allow probation time to review the case and make a recommendation as to what sentence the court should impose. Defendant's request for continuance of the bond until the day of sentencing is hereby granted. If there is nothing further, the court will stand adjourned."

I'm still numb when Leland says to me we'll appeal. I block out everything else he says and just sit there in disbelief. After a few moments, I manage to murmur, "How could they…?"

With microphones stuck in his face, Leland, when asked what he thinks about the verdict, says, "It's a travesty of justice—one for the books." When asked if I plan to appeal the verdict, he says, "Wouldn't you if you were innocent?"

Leland has me remain in the courtroom while he waits for a juror to emerge from the jury room so he can determine why the jury voted the way it did. Fortunately, the reporters and camera crews flock outside to interview Russell. When Leland returns, he says, "Guess who was willing to talk to me?"

"Who?"

"Malcom McCabe, the foreman. He said they were deadlocked seven to five for conviction after the first vote. He said it was only after being given the Allen charge, the five holdouts relented."

"Should have expected as much."

"When I asked him what the most telling evidence was, he said the eyewitness testimony. What persuaded him, he said was when Mrs. Bingham testified she had never had a gun poked in her face before and that the perpetrator's face was forever etched in her memory."

"That was it?"

"McCabe said the testimony about the baseball cap and silver dollars had little bearing. Your proximity to the Bingham mansion and the Glock 17, he said, together with the positive identification were what really persuaded the jury. He said although he was not persuaded by your lack of an alibi, he said there were some who were."

"Did he say anything about motive?"

"Although he didn't mention her name, he said there was one female juror who insisted that behind every great fortune was a great crime and that you struck her as someone who was hungry for power and money."

"Mrs. Hildebrand!"

"Thought she could go either way," Leland says. "Pretty likely she's one of the seven originally voting for a conviction."

"Sounds like I didn't make a very good impression. Guess I should reread Dale Carnegie's book on *How to Win Friends and Influence People.* At least that will give me something to do while I spend the next quarter century behind bars."

"Whoa! Can't believe even the grim Grimsley will throw the book at you on such flimsy evidence. And I'll turn in my license if the Ohio Supreme Court doesn't reverse your conviction."

When I call Carissa, she's already heard the news.

"I got a call from one of the ladies in my Bible study class. Said she just heard it on the local news. She said your bond had been continued and sentencing was not until the sixteenth. Want me to come pick you up?"

"Are you still speaking to me?"

"I think the vow I took was 'until death do us part,' Slugger. I'm on my way."

At the end of the call, I'm relieved that at least Carissa hasn't written me off. I'm not sure about anyone else. I shudder when I think of having to tell my parents. And Carissa's parents? That will be worse than meeting St. Peter."

THERE IS NOTHING TO celebrate this night. When I put off calling my parents, Carissa says, "You need to call them, Monty. After all, this affects their lives, too. It's better they hear it from you."

I nod and pick up the phone. Dad answers on the first ring. "Monty, what took you so long?" Before I have time to respond, he says, "What the hell kind of juries do they have in Ohio anyway? Bubba says you've been convicted on two counts with one being dismissed."

Hearing that from Dad is like sticking a knife in my gut. I can't hold it in any longer and finally let it all out, blubbering like an idiot. Dad remains silent on the other end of the line. Carissa moves next to me and slips her arm around my waist. Her closeness gives me strength to continue. "Guess they believed the eyewitness and disregarded all the evidence or should I say the lack of evidence."

"Hold on, son, your mother is right here." I hear Dad whisper to Mom, "He's pretty fragile, Willa…"

"Monty, we've been worried sick." Just hearing Mom's voice reopens the flood gate and more tears burst forth.

"It's okay, son. We've been crying, too. We were wondering why you didn't let Danny come down and help?"

I've now gained some semblance of control, "My lawyer did everything he could. It wasn't his fault I was convicted."

"Lordy me, what's to say that can't happen to any of us! How do you prove you didn't do what you've been accused of?"

"Exactly! All you can do is say you didn't do it and if you don't have an alibi then you better pack you toothbrush."

"Do you think the Bingham lady was just being spiteful?"

"Our paths had never crossed. I think she honestly believes that I was the intruder. My photograph just happened to be in the wrong place at the wrong time."

"What rotten luck! Wonder what the odds of that happening are?" Dad asks.

"Probably one in a million," I respond. "I just hope with the lack of any evidence to corroborate the eyewitness testimony my conviction will be reversed on appeal. My attorney said my chances of a reversal are better than fifty-fifty."

"Fifty-fifty, huh? What are your chances of being placed on probation or being released on bond pending appeal?"

I smile. Sounds like Dad's been talking to Danny. He's beginning to sound like a lawyer. "My attorney tells me not to count on either one."

THE SATURDAY, MARCH TENTH, twenty-eighteen, edition of the *Cleveland Daily Bugle* reads:

DR. MONTEL RUDLAND FOUND GUILTY ON TWO COUNTS

Dr. Montel Rudland, a prominent physician and former football star, was found guilty of aggravated burglary and aggravated robbery stemming from a break-in of the mansion of heiress Harriett Porter-Bingham on October 13, 2017. The third charge of felony assault was dismissed by presiding Judge Ian Grimsley upon request of the defense because it was deemed to be a lesser included charge of aggravated robbery. The highly publicized case culminated in a unanimous verdict of guilty being rendered late yesterday afternoon.

Dr. Rudland could be sentenced to three to ten years imprisonment on the aggravated burglary charge and a fine up to $20,000. On the aggravated robbery charge, he faces imprisonment of from three to ten years plus a fine up to $20,000. Under Ohio law, five years imprisonment is mandatory since he was armed with a deadly weapon. Sentences on the two crimes could run concurrently or consecutively.

Judge Grimsley granted the defense motion to allow Dr. Rudland to remain on bond pending sentencing. Sentencing is scheduled for March 16, 2018, at 10:00 a.m.

CHAPTER 11
THE SENTENCING

Although I tried to talk Carissa out of being present at the sentencing, she is insistent on being there. We have arranged to have Dr. David Putnam testify in my behalf. He is a senior associate at Talman Medical Center and the one who hired me. We worked out together every Wednesday afternoon at Glenwood Tower's Health Club prior to my arrest. Carissa and I also socialized with him and his wife Debbie, and Jennifer and his youngest daughter Julie are best friends.

The courtroom is jammed with members of the media and curiosity seekers. I ignore the stares and whispers. Leland had prepared me for a five-year mandatory prison sentence. With good time/earned time that sentence could be cut in half. We're shooting (bad term to use considering the charges) for a stay of sentencing pending appeal. Leland refrains from making a prediction.

I'm standing talking with Carissa across the railing as the bailiff hails the arrival of Judge Grimsley with an order for all to stand. I hasten to my seat with tension I've never experienced before.

"Please be seated." Judge Grimsley is somber. Not sure whether that's a good sign or a bad one. Not wanting to make eye contact, I look down.

"Are the parties ready for sentencing?" he asks.

Both Russell and Leland announce that they are.

"The court has a copy of the presentence report provided by the probation department. Mr. Dawson, have you read the report?"

Russell stands. "The prosecution has, Your Honor."

"Mr. Winthrop?"

Leland stands. "The defense has as well, Your Honor."

"Do either of you wish to make any corrections or additions to the recitations or recommendation?"

"No, Your Honor," both Russell and Leland reply.

"The probation department recommends the minimum sentence of five years imprisonment and a five thousand dollar fine for each count to run concurrently. Do either of you disagree with the recommendation?"

Again both Russell and Leland reply "No."

"Does the prosecution have any evidence to present?"

"No, Your Honor. The court is familiar with the evidence from the trial and the factual matters presented in the presentence report. We have nothing further to add."

"Mr. Winthrop?"

"We have a character witness we would like to call."

"Very well, proceed."

"The defense calls Dr. Putnam to the stand."

After Dr. Putnam is called, sworn in and gives his name, address and occupation, Leland asks, "Dr. Putnam, do you know Dr. Monty Rudland, the defendant in this case?"

"I do."

"How is it you know Dr. Rudland?"

"He and I are members of the same medical group, Talman Medical Center here in Cleveland. In fact, I interviewed him and recommended his hiring."

"How long ago was that?"

"Approximately fourteen years."

"I take it you were his mentor—at least to begin with."

"Correct."

"How long have you been affiliated with Talman Medical Center?"

"Approximately twenty years. I was hired right out of residency like Dr. Rudland."

"What year was that?"

"1998. Dr. Rudland was hired in 2004."

"Professionally, how did he handle himself?"

"He was a natural. He probably was the best surgeon in the clinic, and without question, was the most popular among his patients. The feedback on the questionnaires we sent to his patients after treatment was glowing. He was the golden boy, so to speak."

"Did he appear to be honest in his dealings with his patients as well as the clinic?"

"Exemplary on both counts. I'd trust Dr. Rudland with anything I have—including my life."

"Even now?"

"Yes! The jury convicted an innocent and honorable man with absolutely no blemishes on his record, not even a traffic ticket."

"Can you think of an example of his honesty?"

"I could think of a number of them. I'll never forget the first time we played in a golf tournament and he hit the ball in the rough out of sight. When he hit out of the rough onto the green, he told the score keeper to add an extra stroke because he dubbed the ball. That one stroke cost us a tie for the championship."

"Do you think he's capable of burglary, robbery or assault?"

"Not on your life! He was always kind and went out of his way to help people. For example, one day when the weather turned bitter cold, as we headed back from lunch, we passed a vagrant on the street huddling in a doorway shivering from the cold. Dr. Rudland immediately stopped and took off his coat. He then wrapped it around the man and I watched as he pressed a twenty dollar bill into the man's gnarled hand. His random acts of kindness were his trademark."

"What is Dr. Rudland's current status with the Talman Medical Center?"

"He's on administrative leave."

"What is the status of Dr. Rudland's medical license?"

"Upon conviction of a felony, he will likely lose it even though it's not related to the practice of medicine."

"Were you aware he passed the polygraph?"

"Yes, I was told that he had."

"What does that tell you?"

"What I already knew. He did not commit the crimes for which he was charged."

"Would TMC hire him back if it could?"

"Absolutely! No question about it."

"No further questions, Your Honor."

"Mr. Dawson?" Judge Grimsley says and peers down at Russell.

"Yes, Your Honor." Russell stands. "Dr. Putnam, would you change your mind if you knew that Dr. Rudland had been identified by an eyewitness as the perpetrator from both a photographic and a police lineup?"

"No, I would not change my mind. I knew that before coming to court from reading the newspapers and watching newscasts. I also know that a lot of people who have been accused and convicted of crimes on the basis of eyewitness testimony have been exonerated on the basis of DNA and other evidence. I was not aware you had DNA or fingerprint evidence in Dr. Rudland's case."

"We didn't."

"Then how do you know the eyewitness wasn't mistaken?"

"Dr. Putnam," Judge Grimsley interrupts, "as a witness you're to answer questions, not ask them."

"Sorry, Your Honor."

"Hmm," Judge Grimsley says and turns to Russell. "You may continue, Mr. Dawson."

"No further questions, Your Honor."

"Mr. Winthrop, any further questions or other witnesses to call?"

"No, Your Honor."

"Very well." Judge Grimsley clears his throat. "Any argument, Mr. Dawson?"

"No, Your Honor."

"Mr. Wintrhop?"

I could sense Leland's chomping at the bit, and when the judge asks for argument, Leland is instantly on his feet.

"Thank you, Your Honor. Unfortunately, the statute doesn't grant us much leeway when the penalty for aggravated robbery is a minimum of five years in the Ohio State Penitentiary. It doesn't allow consideration for mitigating factors such as those we have in this case. The minimum sentence is the recommendation of the probation department and is not objected to by the prosecution. We still contend the in-court identification of Dr. Rudland by the so-called eyewitness was flawed and that the eyewitness identified the wrong man. Since the jury has spoken, we must abide by the verdict until it is set aside on appeal. And since sentencing is not stayed, we ask for the minimum possible sentence the court can impose. The court has already heard the reasons why that would be fair and just under the circumstances."

"Very well," Judge Grimsley says and turning to me asks, "Dr. Rudland, do you have anything to say in your behalf?"

By his tone, I can tell Judge Grimsley is tiring of our delaying the proceedings and I agonize that if I make a statement, I may incur his wrath. However, I'm entitled to my day in court so I stand as straight as I can when I address the court.

"Your Honor, I've had a lot of challenges in my lifetime but none greater than this. I've done everything I can to prove my innocence. Quite frankly, I'm not sure anyone can prove a negative other than perhaps a polygraph which I have taken and passed. I feel for those unjustly convicted. I also feel for Mrs. Bingham who has been a victim of a crime and is as sure of my guilt as I am of my innocence. To be convicted solely on eyewitness testimony leaves a wide range for error. I can see why my attorney told me at the outset of my case that circumstantial evidence is not just as good as direct evidence but better.

"Your Honor, I remember my grandfather telling me about a man who was accused of cattle rustling. He was hanged from a tree because he was found at the site of a carcass. It was later learned that someone else was the rustler. The rush to judgment cost an innocent man to die, brought unnecessary suffering to his family who were eventually run out of town. I guess I'll have my own story to tell my grandchildren someday.

"I know our system is not perfect. And I don't fault the prosecuting attorney, the jury who found me guilty or you. You all were only doing your job. Nor, do I fault the eyewitness. I just hope someday I can prove her wrong.

"I hope you will take into account the unlikelihood of me being the man who burglarized and robbed Mrs. Bingham when you impose sentence. I didn't commit the crimes for which I have been charged and wouldn't have even if I was starving on the streets. It is not in my genes and not something in my moral makeup. When I swore to tell the truth and said I didn't do it that's something you can take to the bank as my grandfather used to say. As with him, my word is my bond."

There is a hush over the courtroom. I don't cower as I stand waiting for Judge Grimsley to sentence me. If ever there is a time to stand tall, it's now. I'm not the first and won't be the last man who's innocent to be convicted. At least I won't be nailed to the cross and left to die an ignominious death—at least that is my expectation.

"Stay right where you are for the moment, Dr. Rudland, while I determine whether the victim or anyone in her behalf desires to address the court."

"I do," comes a booming voice from the back.

"Come forward, please," Judge Grimsley says as he squints at an imposing figure that emerges from the crowd. I make room for him at the podium.

"Judge," the baritone voice barks in an authoritative manner, "my name is Emmerson Charlesworth. I practice law in New York City and am a family attorney for the Binghams." Charlesworth is dressed in a grey three piece pinstripe suit with an underlying white shirt exposing gold cufflinks accented with diamonds and a colorful Jerry Garcia tie. In the jacket breast pocket is a matching flamboyant pocket square. He looks like he just stepped out of *GQ Magazine.*

"Mr. Charlesworth, welcome to Cleveland," Judge Grimsley smiles and says, "You have the floor."

"Thank you, Judge. I'm here at Mrs. Bingham's request. Unfortunately, she has some health issues that prevent her from being here. I'm her voice."

Wonder if he's a member of the Metropolitan Opera.

"As an attorney for over forty years and a former federal circuit court judge, I find that juries for the most part take their jobs seriously and don't convict unless it is warranted by the evidence.

"Eyewitness testimony, as far as I'm concerned, is still the most reliable, particularly when the eyewitness has no motive to fabricate. And I might add from my experience that most defendants seem to have an excuse or justification for their actions. Either they didn't do it or it was a frame-up or the authorities have the wrong guy. It is always someone else's fault.

"I'm here to vouch for Mrs. Bingham's integrity and to attest to the fact that she is not prone to making mistakes. She also believes no bad deed should go unpunished. She is not seeking vengeance or any kind of retribution. All that she is asking for is a sentence that fits the crimes and because of the aggravated nature of the crimes that a slap on the wrist would be most inappropriate.

"With all the unsolved burglaries in the Cleveland area, your sentence will either send a message that it's okay to violate the law or that criminal conduct will not be tolerated no matter who you are or whether or not you have a criminal record. There is always a first time and by your sentence you can make it the last."

Standing next to a man who wants my head on a platter is not easy. Charlesworth looks me up and down, probably assessing my attire compared to his. I swallow hard as a lump forms in my throat when I watch as Judge Grimsley scratches out something on what I assume is my mittimus and writes something on the form.

"Dr. Rudland," Judge Grimsley says sternly. "I've been torn as to what sentence to impose in light of the severity of the crimes and your otherwise exemplary record. I don't think the minimum is appropriate nor do I think the maximum is either. Therefore, I'm imposing a sentence of imprisonment in the Ohio State Penitentiary for a term of ten years and a fine of ten thousand dollars on each of the counts. The sentences shall run concurrently. Your bond is hereby revoked and you shall be remanded to the custody of the warden of the Ohio State Penitentiary in Youngstown, Ohio, pending the outcome of any appeal. Good luck, Dr. Rudland."

Did he actually say "good luck?" Leland prepared me for the minimum sentence of five years so when I receive ten years I almost collapse. Somewhere behind me, I hear Carissa sob and I can't bear to look at her for fear I'll also break down.

LATER ON I LEARN from Leland that what was crossed out on the mittimus was five years and what was inserted was ten years. It's obvious Judge Grimsley succumbed to public opinion rather than his own best judgment. So much for the recommendation of the probation department. To him it mattered not what the sentence was as long as he received public acclaim.

I'M BEING HELD IN the Cuyahoga County Jail pending my transfer to the Ohio State Penitentiary. The penitentiary is only seventy-five miles from Cleveland. I'm taken from the courtroom to the local jail and I'm not allowed visitors until the following day. Carissa is waiting in the lobby of the jail the next morning. She has with her the morning edition of the *Cleveland Daily Bugle*.

She blows me a kiss through the glass that separates us. I blow her a kiss back. We speak to each other through a phone.

"Still love me?" I ask.

"Do and always will."

"How does it feel to be married to a convict?"

"No different than before."

"You sure?"

"As sure as the world is round and that you're innocent."

"That's what I like about you."

"What's that?" she asks.

"Everything," I blubber. I want to tell her all the reasons but know once I start I'll become a basket case. Her lips quiver and I know she is having a difficult time controlling her emotions.

"Hey," she says, trying to change the conversation, "you made the front page—again." She then holds up the front page of the *Cleveland Daily Bugle* and presses it against the glass. It reads:

DR. RUDLAND RECEIVES TEN YEAR PRISON SENTENCE

Despite the recommendation of the probation department and prosecuting attorney, Russel Dawson, Chief Judge Ian Grimsley on Friday sentenced Dr. Montel Rudland to 10 years imprisonment in the Ohio State Penitentiary and a fine of $10,000 on the aggravated burglary and aggravated robbery charges. The same are to run concurrently.

At the two hour sentencing hearing, where Dr. Rudland's wife was in attendance, Dr. Rudland continued to proclaim his innocence. "I've done everything I can to prove my innocence," he said. "Quite frankly, I'm not sure anyone can prove a negative other than perhaps a polygraph which I have taken and passed. I feel sorry for those unjustly convicted."

When asked by Judge Grimsley whether the victim, heiress Harriett Porter-Bingham, or anyone in her behalf wished to make a statement, Mrs. Bingham's attorney, Emmer-

son Charlesworth, came forward and echoed everything our community wanted to say. "…most defendants seem to have an excuse or justification for their actions. Either they didn't do it or it was a frame-up or the authorities have the wrong guy. It's always someone else's fault."

In vouching for Mrs. Bingham's integrity, Charlesworth, a former circuit court judge from New York, said, "Eyewitness testimony…is still the most reliable particularly where the eyewitness has no motive to fabricate."

The minimum sentence for aggravated robbery (armed robbery) is five-years. That was the sentence recommended by the probation department as well as the prosecution. Pending an appeal, Dr. Rudland will be housed at the Ohio State Penitentiary in Youngstown. It is expected his medical licenses in Ohio and Iowa will be revoked as a result of the two felony convictions. When asked after sentencing if the conviction of Dr. Rudland would result in solving the other burglaries, prosecuting attorney, Russell Dawson, said, "There is absolutely no evidence linking Dr. Rudland to any other crimes."

THE HOUR AND A half trip to Youngstown wouldn't have been so bad if it hadn't been for the handcuffs digging deep into my wrists. That together with no leg room because the front seats had been pushed back as far as they could go made me wonder if this is the way I would be treated for the next ten years. I didn't dare complain because I knew the two officers who transported me were just looking for a way to test their batons.

Once I reached OSP, I was processed and received some rather rough treatment. The guards were not the only ones to call me little rich boy. When I was escorted to my cell, still in cuffs, the taunts continued. "Why didn't you assert the austerity defense?" more than one prisoner yelled. "Couldn't buy your way out?" several said mockingly.

"Not going to make any friends here," I muttered as one of the guards removed my cuffs and shoved me into my cell.

"Don't make no trouble and you'll be just fine," he said, as he locked the cell door.

The penitentiary has a capacity of five hundred and two inmates. My inmate number is an even five hundred.

THE FIRST NIGHT IN prison was probably the worst. There was quite a bit of banging on the bars and lots of expletives being bantered around the cellblock. When I finally fell asleep on my bunk, I was abruptly awakened by an inmate who, apparently, could no longer tolerate his man-sized bird cage existence. In his anxiety, and needing a fix no doubt, he threw what I would call a temper tantrum. He began yelling and screaming and banging his head against the bars. The guards placed him in a strait jacket still yelling and screaming. He was then dragged by two burly guards past my cell out of the cellblock. So much for my first night at OSP.

In the morning, the doors opened automatically. We lined up in the corridor and were escorted to the mess hall where the food was served cafeteria style. Though most of the breakfast was processed food, there were some fresh bananas. I was told later that bananas were a rarity. I didn't complain. The option, I learned later, was to purchase nutritional food from the commissary.

When I got back to my cell, I found I had a roommate. Jose and I hit it off from the beginning. Both of us had been convicted of aggravated robbery. Since he was fifty pounds lighter than me, he agreed to sleep on the upper bunk.

At breakfast the next morning, Jose and I found an isolated corner to sit in. We were shunned by the other inmates. This reminded me of the ranch. When a new horse was introduced into a corral with other horses, the newbie received some rather harsh treatment and was ostracized by the other horses. With Jose in the picture, I at least had someone to have meals with.

I had been at OSP for less than two weeks when a stabbing occurred in the prison yard. The prisoner/victim was bleeding profusely. I moved the crowd back and used my handkerchief and a twig to make a tourniquet and stopped the bleeding. I stayed with the victim and monitored him until medical help arrived on the scene. Although I knew it, I was later told if the victim had not received immediate treatment he would have bled to death. From that point forward, I was heralded a hero and became part of the club. Now everyone wanted to sit by Jose and me, and finding out I was a medical doctor, I was sought out by anyone and everyone with a malady or medical problem ranging from a headache to the flu. Eventually, I was helping with patients in the prison infirmary.

Carissa spent as much time visiting me as she could and was always encouraging. She would relate the news regarding Jayden, Jennifer, Paxton and her parents and leave a handful of quarters for the very pricey snacks in the prison vending machines. Leland would also drive the seventy-five miles to assist in the appeal and after it was filed to keep me updated.

He never abandoned me. He also spent as much time as he could talking about politics, sports, world events and religion. He made it clear that he was not charging me for anything post-trial. He was very encouraging about our chances on appeal and I was impressed by his appellate skills. His first time in court was before the Ohio Supreme Court, a case he won. And he appeared not long after that in the United States Supreme Court, a case he also won. I felt fortunate to have him in my corner. Leland and Carissa made prison more bearable.

EPILOGUE

Thursday, May thirty-first, twenty-eighteen, was another day I will always remember. I had just returned from the prison infirmary after having performed an emergency appendectomy on a prisoner. His appendix had ruptured and the prison doctor had been unavailable. The warden was aware that my license had been revoked but said if I didn't perform the surgery, the prisoner would die. It was the lesser of evils and I went ahead with the surgery, saving the prisoner's life. *What else can they do to me, revoke my license—again?*

When the warden came to my cell, I thought it was about the patient. "Unlock Dr. Rudland's cell," he ordered. "We're gonna miss you around here," he said to me.

"Wha… What do you mean?" I said. "Am I being transferred already?"

"Your attorney is here with some news he shared with me. He's waiting in my office."

What the hell's going on… then it dawned on me, I must have won my appeal. "I won my appeal!" I blurted.

"Better than that!" was all the warden would tell me.

After all I'd endured from the beginning of the ordeal, I was reluctant to get my hopes up. What could possibly be better than winning my appeal?

When I enter the warden's office, Leland jumps up. There are tears in his eyes.

"Mon…Monty," he manages to say.

"Yes…," I say, in an anxious voice.

"I cancelled a court hearing to tell you the news in person." By now he's grinning from ear to ear. The last hour and a half has been the longest hour and a half in my life."

For crying out loud, forget the theatrics and just spit it out!

"Russell, as we speak, is preparing a writ of habeas corpus to obtain your release and appearance in Grimsley's court."

I suddenly have a flashback of the last time I appeared in Grimsley's court and cringe at the thought of going back there. *How can this be good news?*

Leland continues, "Russell is also preparing a motion to withdraw the mittimus and dismiss your case with prejudice which means it can never be filed again."

I stagger and collapse onto one of the chairs. "Why the sudden change of heart? The appeal?"

"The appeal has nothing to do with it." Warden Cameron is still standing there and seems to be enjoying the conversation.

"What then?" I squint, still wondering what the hell is going on.

Before Leland can reply, Warden Cameron interrupts. "Why don't the two of you go into the conference room where you can be alone?"

After he closes the door, Leland is like a kid who can't wait to divulge a secret.

"Mrs. Bingham was hospitalized recently with some kind of recurring ailment. She was taken to St. Clements, the same place she was hospitalized during the first part of October of last year about ten days prior to the break-in. Anyway, during the course of her stay, she spotted an orderly she thought was you. Her attorney, Emmerson Charlesworth, was visiting her at the time. Mrs. Bingham became so enraged she had to be sedated. She insisted Charlesworth immediately contact the prosecuting attorney and find out why you had been released from prison. Even though she was assured you were still in prison, she insisted someone immediately come to the hospital and see for themselves.

"To make a long story short, Detectives Summers and Reynolds, together with an investigator from the prosecutor's office went to St. Clements, if for no other reason than to satisfy Mrs. Bingham that her claim that she saw you was wrong. Upon interviewing other hospital personnel, the detectives found out the orderly in question was a man by the name of Philip Hacking, and it just so happened he was on duty at the time the detectives arrived. Checking personnel records, they also learned Hacking was employed by St. Clements during the spree of burglaries. Reynolds then had one of the nurses escort him to Hacking's station, and upon seeing the orderly, it is said that Reynolds gasped—he was a dead ringer for you."

I'm sitting there dumbfounded. I can't believe what I'm hearing.

"The orderly was taken into custody. It turned out he had an extensive criminal record. It also turned out his fingerprints matched prints taken at various burglary scenes. Why they didn't turn up in the data base, I don't know. If they had, his mug shot would have been in the photographic lineup Mrs. Bingham reviewed instead of yours. In fact, if the police had done their job right, he would have been jailed long before the break-in at the Bingham mansion and you wouldn't be sitting here today."

I find it hard to rejoice that after I've been completely destroyed, the real burglar is found. *Guess I should be thankful he was uncovered before I served any more of my sentence.*

"How was it he was able to pull off all these burglaries and particularly the burglary I was charged with having committed?"

"Apparently, car keys along with house keys and other valuables were stored for safe keeping in a room at St. Clements that resembled a mailroom. The mini-lockers where the keys and other valuables were kept were numbered. The numbers were designated on a master list with the names of the patients to whom the keys belonged. By pulling the file with the patient's name, which Hacking had access to, he could determine the patient's address. He also had access to the master key for the lockers."

"Don't tell me," I say. "When he matched the key to the address he made a house call."

"Something like that. So that the keys wouldn't be missed, he took them to a hardware store where his cousin worked and had duplicates made. When he thought the time was right and the patient was not at home, he made his raid."

I lean back in my chair, "Sounds as though he confessed."

"According to Russell, he did. In fact, they hit the jackpot. He confessed not only to the crimes you were charged with but to all the other burglaries."

"So the authorities have his confession, Mrs. Bingham's account and identification as well as his fingerprints from the prior burglaries."

"Yep," Russell says. When they executed a search warrant of his residence, they turned up a lot of items taken in the various burglaries, including several handguns, one of which matched the description Mrs. Bingham gave police."

"How about the other incriminating evidence, such as the Cleveland Indians baseball cap and the three worn silver dollars?"

"He mentioned both the baseball cap and the three worn silver dollars minted in the 1890s were seized. He said they also found keys, including one that had a tag with Mrs. Bingham's address attached to it."

"Does that mean I'm off the hook?"

"As soon as you're brought before the court and Russell makes the appropriate motions and Judge Grimsley grants them, you will be."

I nod. "What day is this?"

"Memorial Day, May twenty-eighth," Leland responds, "a day of remembrance."

"Of course, I should have known," I say. "I knew you wouldn't abandon me."

"Nor has your wife or your friends."

It then occurs to me, "Does Carissa know?"

"I told Bethany and she told her."

"Praise God," I say. "Miracles do happen. I guess all you have to do is pray for them."

WHEN I RETURN TO the Cuyahoga County Courthouse, Carissa is waiting for me outside the courtroom. She is all smiles. I'm being escorted to the holding cell by sheriff's officers, however I manage to say to her as we pass, "Meet you in the courtroom."

The press mulls around in confusion, acting like they don't know what's going on. *Serves 'em right.* Before long I'm taken into the courtroom.

I'm wearing prison orange with Ohio State Penitentiary stenciled on the back, handcuffs and shackles. I walk like a penguin as I make my way to the ever familiar defense table where Leland is sitting. Spotting me, he stands, smiles and hugs me.

Our encounter is being captured on the cellphones of the reporters. I turn and wink at Carissa. She winks back.

When the clerk enters the courtroom, she immediately heads for the deputies and whispers something to them. Soon my handcuffs and shackles are removed. Shortly thereafter, the bailiff orders all to stand as Judge Grimsley enters. I notice his presence is not as imposing as before. In fact, he's somewhat subdued. He calls the case of *The People of the State of Ohio v. Montel Rudland.*

"Let the record reflect that the prosecution is represented by Russell Dawson and Dr. Rudland is present with his attorney, Leland Winthrop."

Spotting Carissa, he asks, "Are you Dr. Rudland's wife?"

Carissa nods.

"Welcome," Judge Grimsley says to Carissa.

"This matter comes before the court on a writ of habeas corpus I issued earlier today. Mr. Dawson, your office has filed a motion to vacate the mittimus remanding Dr. Rudland to the custody of the warden of the Ohio State Penitentiary to serve a ten-year sentence on aggravated burglary and aggravated robbery charges. You have also asked that the judgments on the two verdicts be withdrawn and all charges against Dr. Rudland be dismissed with prejudice meaning they can never be revived."

Russell stands and says, "We have, Your Honor."

"For the record, and for the benefit of all here present, please state the grounds for your motion."

"Mrs. Bingham, the victim and eyewitness in the case at bar, has recanted her identification of Dr. Rudland and identified another man, one with an extensive criminal history, who has confessed to having committed the crimes for which Dr. Rudland has been charged, convicted and sentenced."

When all hell breaks loose in the courtroom, an enraged Judge Grimsley jumps up and bangs his gavel cracking the glass top of the bench and shouts, "Any further outbursts and I'll have all of you removed from the courtroom." The stern look on Judge Grimsley's face says everyone better comply. When the mayhem subsides, he says to Russell, "Mr. Dawson, please proceed."

"The actual perpetrator is now in custody and matches the description Mrs. Bingham gave police shortly after the incident to a T, including having brown eyes unlike Dr. Rudland, whose eyes are blue. The actual perpetrator's residence was searched and the infamous Cleveland Indians baseball cap, three worn silver dollars minted in the 1890s and a handgun matching the one used in the crimes were seized along with a key with a tag marked with Mrs. Bingham's address."

"According to the motion you submitted, Mr. Dawson, the actual perpetrator, as you refer to him, confessed not only to the break-in on October thirteenth, twenty-seventeen, at Mrs. Bingham's mansion but to the other break-ins in and around the area." Judge Grimsley sets down the motion and peering over his glasses at Russell, asks, "Is that correct, Mr. Dawson?"

"It is, Your Honor." Russell looks at me and smiles. All of a sudden he's in my corner. After what he did to me, I don't feel real friendly toward him—too little, too late.

Judge Grimsley begins signing several documents including, I assume, an order granting the prosecution's motion. Without looking up, he asks, "Any objection to the motion, Mr. Winthrop?"

"Absolutely none, Your Honor," Leland says.

"Very well then, gentlemen, the court has signed an order granting the motion to vacate the judgment of guilty heretofore entered in this cause and has entered an order dismissing all charges brought against Dr. Rudland with prejudice. The court has also signed an order vacating the mittimus heretofore entered herein and hereby orders the release of Dr. Rudland from the custody of the warden of the Ohio State Penitentiary."

Judge Grimsley beckons the clerk who, when she comes forward, is handed the signed orders. "Here, fax these to the warden of the Ohio State Penitentiary."

Looking at Leland, Judge Grimsley asks, "Mr. Winthrop, have you prepared an order for me to sign expunging the criminal record including the arrest associated with the prosecution of Dr. Rudland?"

"We have," Leland says. "May I approach?"

"You may."

Leland hands the order to Judge Grimsley who ceremoniously scribbles his signature on the form. "Both sides will be provided with conformed copies of all the orders after we adjourn," Judge Grimsley says.

Some of the reporters are already scrambling to meet their publication deadlines. The others are texting on their iPhones. I take the opportunity to look back at Carissa. She returns my smile as she dabs at her eyes.

I don't know how to feel or what to think. I don't have time to react before Judge Grimsley addresses me. When he says, "Dr. Rudland," I stand in my prison garb albeit without the handcuffs and shackles. For some inexplicable reason I don't feel embarrassed or inhibited. I stand as tall as I can in a jumpsuit that is way too small for me.

"How do you feel about what has just happened here today? You have been exonerated and your record wiped clean." He peers at me with a grim expression, one that seems more contrived than real.

Grimsley acts like he's doing me a favor, and after changing the five-year sentence recommended by the probation department to ten years, I begin to seethe under my jail garb.

Before I can speak, he says, "You can come to the podium if you wish." As I do so, I collect my thoughts.

I've harbored resentment for his bias against me from day one. Now that I have the opportunity to speak my piece, I no longer fear being held in contempt.

"Your Honor, the only way I can answer your question is by asking you one. And you don't have to answer if you wish. How would you feel if our roles were reversed and you were the one standing in my place? I had a thriving medical practice, living the dream with my family and associating with my friends in a location I thought would be my home forever. I was the golden boy at the clinic, at my home, in my neighborhood and in the eyes of everyone who knew me. Perhaps I should write a book entitled 'My Nine Months of Hell' or if my innocence hadn't been determined, 'My Ten Years in a Human-Sized Bird Cage.'

"I compare myself to that famous storybook character Humpty Dumpty when, after his great fall, was unable to put all the pieces back together again. When you finish court at the end of the day, you will go back to a familiar environment—one that is the same as when you left it this morning. You will still have your license to practice law, your appointment as a judge, the respect of your peers and the prestige of your position. Me, when you bid me good luck in a few moments, I will return to an empty house, a defrocked physician whose license to practice medicine in two states has been revoked, whose friends have scattered since his arrest and who is shunned by his peers and neighbors alike.

"Will things be the same going forward? Hardly. I bear the scars of a judicial system that has failed me. A system where a mere accusation is tantamount to a conviction. I was branded as a criminal on the say-so of a witness whose identification was flawed and the presumption of guilt remained with me until I could prove my innocence—something that was impossible to do. But for the subsequent identification of the actual perpetrator by a so-called eyewitness who said she could 'never forget that face,' I would languish in prison for what to me would be an eternity."

Judge Grimsley sits for a few moments glaring at me after I finish my diatribe. He then slams his gavel and announcing, "Court is adjourned!" bolts out through his private exit.

Carissa rushes to the podium where I'm still standing, obviously in shock that I had the guts to say what I did. She slides her arm around my waist, "Hey, Slugger! You hit a home run!"

ABOUT THE AUTHORS

JUDITH BLEVINS' WHOLE professional life has been centered in and around the courts and the criminal justice system. Her experience in having been a court clerk and having served under five consecutive district attorneys in Grand Junction, Colorado, has provided the fodder for her novels. She has had a daily dose of mystery, intrigue and courtroom drama over the years and her novels share all with her readers.

CARROLL MULTZ, A trial lawyer for over forty years, a former two-term district attorney, assistant attorney general, and judge, has been involved in cases ranging from municipal courts to and including the United States Supreme Court. His high profile cases have been reported in the *New York Times*, *Redbook Magazine* and various police magazines. He was one of the attorneys in the Columbine Copycat Case that occurred in Fort Collins, Colorado, in 2001 that was featured by Barbara Walters on ABC's *20/20*. Now retired, he is an Adjunct Professor at Colorado Mesa University in Grand Junction, Colorado, teaching law-related courses at both the graduate and undergraduate levels.